MASQUERADE

MADELEINE TAYLOR

Edited by Claire Jarrett

Cover design by Meg Sayers

1

I'm a little nervous as I follow my friend Tessa past the long rows of enormous properties that make up the Garden District in New Orleans. She insisted we come here tonight and although I was excited while we were shopping for our costumes and masks this afternoon, my normally self-assured demeanor is starting to crumble now that I'm about to enter a party in a city that I only stepped foot in last night and where I don't know anyone apart from Tessa.

"These houses are out of this world," I murmur, peeking through the gates to admire the huge yards and pristine pools. "Are you sure we're dressed appropriately?"

"Are you serious? You look fabulous, Ivy." The masked party being thrown in her friend's huge house is supposed to be the place to be tonight and we've gone all out, following the 'Black & White masquerade' dress code printed on the formal invitation.

"Thank you. So do you." I stare down at my long, black dress and decide that I do indeed, look fabulous. It's vintage and has lace trumpet sleeves that match the skirt part. The black corset I'm wearing over it makes me look a little gothic, and in combination with my black Venetian style feathered mask, long, dark hair and naturally pale face I could very well pass for a ghost in the dark. "And I can't believe how fast you've managed to make friends, considering you only moved here just over five weeks ago."

"What can I say, people are just naturally drawn to me." Tessa bats her eyelashes at me before she pulls her mask over her face, letting me know we're close. She's wearing a white dress we found in the same store. With her blonde hair and white feather adorned mask, we're quite the pair, and passers-by are staring at us from a restaurant terrace as we turn a corner looking like ballerinas about to audition for the leads in *Swan Lake*.

"This one?" I ask incredulously as she stops in front of a huge house that looks stunning and even grander than the pastel-colored French colonial buildings next door.

"Yeah, I think this is it," Tessa says, checking the details.

"How can you not be sure? I thought you knew..." I take the elegantly designed invitation from her and read the name of the host. "Countess Montgomery, which I assume is an alias."

"Knowing is a strong word," Tessa says as the heavy cast-iron gates open, and we're asked by the security team to step into the front yard. An enchanting fountain sits on the lawn to our right. It's lit up from below, the five cherubs in the middle shooting jets of water through their raised trumpets. The beautiful mansion is painted white with pastel green windowsills and shutters. A wide balcony with ornate railings runs along the second floor with French doors painted in the same shade of green. Large trees covered in Spanish moss are lined up on both sides of the long driveway that leads to the front door, and the many lanterns in the trees make for a spectacular sight.

A dozen or so women who have just arrived are hanging out by the gates. Some are wearing suits, but most of them are dressed in skimpy dresses, or very little but an elaborate mask and elegant lingerie with a separate train or a tuxedo jacket. Although they've all respected the black and white theme, their outfits are a lot more daring than ours, and I'm starting to wonder if we got the dress code wrong.

Studying the guests, I make a second observation and voice it. "I don't see any men here." Not that I mind; men are not my thing and I'm here to have some fun.

"You're right. I think we may be in luck tonight." Tessa smirks. "It's been a while since I've been to a women-only party."

My eyes are drawn to a woman in a short, black latex dress, smoking a cigarette under one of the trees by the gates. She's wearing a mask that looks like lead has melted over half her face; silver wax-like drips run down her dark cheeks to complete the effect, but I can see from what's exposed that she's very pretty. Wild curls frame her mahogany face, and the mask accentuates her full lips. Another woman joins her wearing a sharp-tailored black suit. She has short, slicked back dark hair and is wearing a distinctly shaped *Phantom of the Opera* mask. Her eyes are so black that I wonder if she's wearing contacts as she stares at me, sizing me up like prey. It's giving me chills, yet I can't help but look at her, too.

"Good evening," Tessa says, flashing the invitation at one of the female security guards.

"Good evening." A woman the size of a tree looks down at Tessa and raises a brow. "Password?"

I glance at Tessa, whose eyes flash back and forth between me, the talking tree and the street behind us. "It's ehm..." Tessa shuffles on the spot, then lets out a deep sigh. "Fuck."

I groan at her, because by now, I know exactly what's going on. "Where did you get that invitation from?" I whisper at her. "Be honest. It's clear you weren't invited."

"I found it," Tessa says in a thin voice, looking deflated as her shoulders drop. "On the floor of the public restrooms, in the hotel I was staying at before I got the keys to my apartment."

"No password, no entry," the tree-like woman says in a friendly but pressing tone, gesturing to the gates for us to leave.

"I can't believe you pulled this on me again," I mumble in embarrassment, remembering New Year's Eve, the last time she falsely claimed to have been invited to an exclusive party in New York, where we both lived at the time. "I'm thirty-five and you've made me try to crash a party for the second time in a year. It's embarrassing beyond belief."

Tessa doesn't reply, clearly mortified herself, but just as we're about to leave, the woman in the suit walks up to us. "Wait, they're with me," she says to the security guard before taking my hand, bending forward and kissing the top of it. Her lips press so softly against my skin that I can barely feel it, yet a shiver runs through me as I watch her bow. Something about her is incredibly sensual, and I'm curious to know what's behind the mask.

"Miss...?" Her voice is low and husky.

"Miss Black," I lie, not feeling entirely comfortable giving my surname to a stranger, even if the stranger has just saved us from humiliation.

"Welcome to the party, Miss Black." The woman turns to Tessa. "Then you must be Miss White?" An amused smile plays around her lips. "Are you... together?"

"No," I'm quick to say, unsure why I desperately want her to know I'm single. Tessa is my ex, but our attraction faded over twelve years ago and we've been best friends ever since. We recently agreed during a drunken night that we'd rather chew our arms off than sleep with each other again, so there's never even been as much as a flirty comment between us since we were in our early twenties.

"Good." The woman's smile widens. "Let me introduce myself. In case you hadn't worked it out I'm the Phantom, and this is my friend Stephanie," she says when the woman in the latex dress joins us. "Stephanie, will you show Miss White to the bar, please? I'll make sure Miss Black gets a drink." She holds out her arm and instinctively I hook mine through it as I glance at Tessa, who is being whisked away by the other woman.

I can't say I'm entirely comfortable around the Phantom, as she calls herself; she's persistent, acting as if she's already got me in her pocket, and I'm aware of the heavy gates closing behind me. When I observe guests entering the mansion, I note that they have a strange air about them, and that the atmosphere is way darker than I expected. The idea of finding Tessa and sneaking out after one drink crosses my mind, but first, I need to apologize. "I'm terribly sorry about gate-crashing the party," I say, looking up at her. "My friend told me she knew the hostess, but that's clearly not the case."

"Don't worry about it." My handsome companion takes a tighter hold of my arm as she leads me to the entrance. "I know most people here and you're with me, now. I couldn't have wished for a better surprise than a gorgeous stranger showing up unexpectedly, so please allow me the pleasure of your company, at least for a little while."

2

"Cocktail?" The Phantom hands me a tall glass with a black liquid that smells faintly of licorice. "There's champagne at the other bar if you prefer, but I thought this suited your looks tonight."

"Thank you." I take a sip and let it roll over my palette. "It's good."

"Of course." She says it as if it's a given that anything this party has to offer is good. "It has a couple of secret ingredients, but don't worry—it's all natural."

"Are you telling me the drinks are spiked?" I raise a brow at her and tilt my head.

"No. I'm saying the cocktail contains certain herbs. There's nothing synthetic in there and it won't make you go crazy or do anything you don't want to do." She winks. "It might enhance your desires, though."

As her words linger between us, I contemplate handing the drink back and leaving, but I can't seem to tear myself away from her. She has an air about her that draws me in, and I find her incredibly attractive. In desperate need of liquid courage, and for no reason other than that my intuition tells me it's okay, I decide to trust her and take another sip. "Very well, I'll take your word for it."

I must admit, the place looks very, very impressive as she offers her arm and shows me around. Two bars are set up in the spacious living room that is dimly lit and decorated with antique furniture, rich tapestries, huge chandeliers and exquisite, old oil paintings. Despite the opulence, I can see that the furniture is worn-out, and that there has been little maintenance done in the past years. It must be terribly expensive to maintain a house like this, but the paintwork that is chipped in places and the slightly damaged wallpaper, only adds to the charm.

The scent of incense hangs thick in the air and my sight is blurred by the occasional clouds of mist coming from the dry ice machine behind the DJ booth, which is set up in a corner of the room. An androgynous looking woman dressed in nothing but a pair of black shorts and a tuxedo jacket, is playing a slow, eerie tune that adds to the mysterious, laid-back vibe. In the middle of the room, the furniture has been cleared, and women are slow dancing, which is something I haven't done since my high school graduation party.

People are everywhere, loitering on the sweeping staircase that leads up from the grand hallway and we spot others in various rooms as we pass their open doorways. The staff hired for tonight are dressed in simple black suits and black masks, and it's kind of intriguing not being able to see anyone's faces. Perhaps my companion is the most intriguing of all; her nonchalance and total confidence making me more and more curious by the minute. She's clearly interested in me too, as she hasn't taken her intense black eyes off me for a second and is blatantly ignoring everyone else.

"So, does the Phantom have a first name?" I ask.

She tilts her head and takes a sip of her drink, and her smile sends shivers down my spine. "Not tonight. Tonight, I'm just the Phantom."

"Right." I chuckle. "So, is *The Phantom of the Opera* your favorite musical?"

"Not quite."

"Okay," I say, wondering why it's so damn hard to get any information out of this woman. She's clearly not one for small talk. "Well, my name is..."

"Shh..." She hushes me, placing her thumb on my lips and it's making me tingle all over. "Don't you like the anonymity we've got going on here?" She leans in closer to whisper in my ear. "Don't you like the idea of having a mind-blowing night with a stranger who will please you in ways you can't even begin to imagine?"

Her last question makes me take in a quick breath, and as my lips part, she keeps her thumb there, wedging it between them. It sets me on fire and parts of me that have been neglected in the past year suddenly come to life, reminding me of what I've been missing. I can't say the thought of kissing her hasn't crossed my mind in the ten minutes I've spent in her company. Her lips are alluring, and her eyes have something dark and dangerous about them that arouses me each time she looks at me. Sex with a stranger is not something I'd normally even consider, but still, I make no effort to remove her thumb. Quite the opposite; I fight the urge to suck it into my mouth, and when she straightens herself and pulls her hand away, I feel a flicker of disappointment.

"I don't know what to say to that."

"But it's simple." Again, there's that stare. "Does that idea turn you on, or not?" Awaiting my answer, she takes my drink from me and puts it down before she pulls me in by my waist, drawing me against her. "Never mind, where are my manners? I should at least offer you a dance to give you time to think about it."

I'm grateful for the dancefloor as I'm not sure I can manage to hold a conversation after her indecent proposal, so I let her lead the way.

"Do you know how masked balls started?" she asks, pressing her hand firmly into the small of my back.

"No," I whisper, aware of the alarming lack of distance between our lips. "Tell me." I'm not a great dancer and I have no idea what I'm doing, but it doesn't matter. There's music, we're moving, and our physical closeness feels amazing. It's been a while since I've felt a woman's body against my own, and hers does not disappoint. Strong arms, her thigh brushing between my legs each time she takes a step forward, her hips against mine...

"Balls have a long history, but masks were first worn during carnival season, where big indulgent celebrations were held before Lent; generally seen as a time of somber fasting," the Phantom says. "People wore masks to hide their identity, so they could drink as much as they wanted, express controversial opinions and even have sex with people from different social classes, without having to face the consequences. Masks gave them the anonymity they needed to be free. Eighteenth-century masked balls were especially of an erotic nature." She pauses, and her lips pull into a smile. "I feel like indulging tonight. Do you?"

"I think I do," I hear myself say, but I'm not sure if I mean it. Although my body wants to, from the way it's reacting to her, it seems a little extreme for me. I came here with the intention of maybe meeting some new people, to have some fun, to flirt a little but not to dive under the covers with a stranger.

Scanning the crowd and simultaneously searching for Tessa, I notice a lot of people are making out and, in some cases, it's getting very heated. Considering it's not even ten pm, I doubt any of these people are too drunk to realize what they're doing. There's a voyeuristic atmosphere, as if by some silent understanding, it's okay for them to do whatever they want here tonight. "What kind of party is this?" I ask, not sure if I'm ready for the answer.

"The fun kind. The hedonistic kind." The Phantom moves her hand lower, so that she can caress my behind and she then roughly squeezes it. "Are you okay with that?"

I bite my lip and nod, then realize what I've just done and shake my head. "Not my scene," I say, still drawn to her mouth. It's like I can't take my eyes off her lips, and I'm dying to know what's under the mask. Her short hair is gelled back, the way a fifties salesman would wear it, or perhaps phantoms, if they were real.

"Then you shouldn't have gate-crashed." She winks, letting me know she's joking. "If you want me to walk you out, I will, but I can't help thinking it would be a waste of a wonderful opportunity for both of us."

I choose not to answer, buying myself time. Finally, I spot Tessa on a chaise in the corner of the room, talking to Stephanie. They're sitting next to each other and Stephanie already has her arm around her. Seeing how engaged Tessa looks, I know that I won't be able to drag her away from the woman if I try, but I have a spare key to her apartment, so it doesn't really matter. I'll leave when I want to leave, I tell myself, although I'm not totally sure what I really want regarding anything at this point. My seductive temptress of a phantom has planted a seed in my mind, and I keep wondering what it would feel like if she kissed me.

The song comes to an end, and the Phantom takes my hand and leads us back to the bar. "How about another drink, Miss Black?"

3

———

"So, what do people talk about without giving anything away about themselves?" I ask when we're sitting on a couch in something that looks like a reception room. There are fewer people in here, but the vibe is the same; steamy, heated, sexual. No one is taking it any further than kissing so far, but their hands have started to wander now, and it's hard not to look. "I can't ask you about your name, how you know the hostess, or what you do for a living," I continue, desperate to take my mind off the woman opposite me, whose hand is now making its way up another woman's thigh.

"We could talk about what you'd like me to do to you in bed," she suggests matter-of- factly, making my heart rate go up so fast that I clutch onto my chest. "I take it from your reaction that public intimacy isn't your thing, but I have a nice room upstairs. Countess Montgomery is fine with me using it and it's very private."

"Of course you do." I can't help but laugh because she's simply not giving up. After my second drink though, I'm feeling more relaxed and the chemistry between us is explosive.

"Well?" She arches a brow. "What do you want, Miss Black?"

A blush rises to my cheeks and I hide behind my glass. Being a professional nightclub singer, I'm not normally the shy retiring type, but I seem to have lost my ability to speak tonight. "I'm not sure if I know what I want. Not right now, anyway."

My seductress nods, the corners of her mouth tugging up. "Then maybe you should let me decide what you want. Do you like handing over control?"

"What do you mean by that?"

"You know very well what I mean. Does the idea of me being in command appeal to you?"

"No." As the answer leaves my lips in a breathy whimper, I know I'm lying. Although I've had many fantasies, I've never submitted to anyone. "Maybe."

"Maybe means you're curious. Are you curious, Miss Black?" Her eyes flash back at me and I let out a quiet breath before I finally give in.

"Yes."

It's just one word, but somehow, I feel like that one word is about to change my world. A rush of heat spreads between my thighs, making me quiver. Clearly, I want this more that I realized, and if I'm ever going to try something totally out of my comfort zone, it might as well be with an anonymous stranger who I will never see again.

"Are you sure?" Her hand slides up my thigh, making my chest heave. "You know what? It doesn't matter; you can change your mind anytime." A gentle squeeze is all the encouragement I need, because all I can think of now is having that hand in other places. I have no idea how she's done it, but within the span of an hour, I've agreed to go upstairs with her and let her do God knows what to me.

"Yes, I'm sure."

"Then let's explore together." Taking my glass from me, the Phantom stands up and holds out her hand. "Let me show you to the room."

My legs are trembling as I get up, but deep down, I know I'll regret it if I don't do this tonight. I told Tessa earlier I was ready to have some fun again, after my girlfriend left me for someone else eight months ago, and this woman is not only devilishly attractive and charming, but the sexual chemistry is like nothing I've ever felt before. My body is craving to be touched again, and her fleeting caresses and dark eyes have set me on fire. "Wait... I need to check on Tessa."

"I have no doubt she's enjoying herself." The Phantom leads me to the living room, where I see Tessa making out with Stephanie in a big armchair. She's draped half on top of her and she seems to have been sucked into the same sexual energy as everyone else. It's typical Tessa, throwing herself into the arms of the first woman who pays her attention—she's always been that way—but Stephanie is smoking hot and I'm happy for her. Besides, I'm in no position to judge her as I'm about to do exactly the same thing myself.

"Tessa," I say, gently nudging her shoulder.

"Oh, hey." Tessa looks from me to Stephanie and back as if I've just woken her up from a spell. Realizing her bra is visible, she frowns and pulls the shoulder strap of her dress back up. "Are you okay?"

"Yeah. I'll just be gone for a bit. Do you mind?"

Glancing down at Stephanie, she grins before she turns back to me. "No, I don't mind. I'll be right here if you need me."

"Are you okay?" I have to ask, because even for her, this is unusual behavior. "Do you feel weird in any way?"

"No. I feel…" Tessa takes a moment to think about it, then says, "I just feel immensely turned on, that's all." Then Stephanie pulls her back toward her mouth and they fall into another heated kiss like I'm not even there.

The Phantom doesn't seem to think this is strange at all, and judging by the situation in the room, I know we need to either leave or join in, being the only voyeurs among many heated bodies. Groups have started to form naturally, a mysterious organic attraction pulling women together and I can see where this is heading. Concluding Tessa is fine, I take a deep breath and give my new friend a look that tells her I'm ready.

We walk up two flights of the broad staircase and head for a door at the end of the corridor. There's nothing but silence between us, but it's not uncomfortable. On the contrary—it only adds to the excitement and anticipation that is growing inside of me. I've just surrendered to my fate for the night, even though I have no idea what will happen. She takes a key out of her pocket and unlocks the door. "After you."

4

"Are you sure someone lives in this house?" I take a
minute to let my eyes adjust to the dark while the
Phantom lights the candles on the nightstands, then locks
the door and leaves the key in the lock. "It looks like an old
man's room; I can't imagine a countess living here," I add. I
know for sure this will not be the last of the many silly
things to slip from my tongue tonight, as my mind seems to
unravel when I'm nervous, and right now, I'm very, very
nervous.

She seems amused by my comment and laughs. "Yes, I'm
sure. She hasn't done much to the house in the past twenty
years. But yes, now that you've mentioned it; it does look like
an old man's room."

A big, four-poster mahogany bed dominates the room,
Victorian I think, but I know nothing about furniture so I
can't be sure. There's an antique rocking chair in one corner,
a tall closet and a matching dressing table standing against
the walls, and a Persian rug covers most of the floor. Old
family portraits hang against the ornamental wallpaper,
whilst heavy velvet drapes are pulled back, letting in a little

streetlight. Anyone catching a glimpse of me standing in front of the window right now would be freaked out, especially by the way I'm dressed tonight, looking like a lost ghost in this big house.

I gesture to something that is covered by a white sheet, standing on the dressing table. "What's that?"

My masked companion looks at the sheet and purses her lips as if seeing it for the first time. "Just a mirror. I don't like them."

Her answer throws me, because it's weird, and I study her as she closes the distance between us. "Are you scared of mirrors?" I'm trying to remember if I saw any downstairs, but I don't think I did.

She ignores my question and trails a hand down my cheek. I reach out to take off her mask, but she stops me. "No. My mask stays on."

"Why?" I don't object, but at the same time many things go through my mind. Is she hiding something behind the mask that she doesn't want me to see? Is that why she doesn't like mirrors? Is she worried her appearance will disappoint me? She doesn't seem insecure in the slightest, so it doesn't make sense. I decide it makes no difference to me because by now I'm so turned on that I wouldn't care if she had a third eye between her brows. When I reach out again, she catches my wrist.

"No, Miss Black. As I said, the mask stays on. In this room, we play by my rules and that's how it's going to be tonight." She pauses, her dark eyes meeting mine. "If you're uncomfortable with that, I understand. The key is in the lock so you can leave anytime you want. But if you want me to make you feel really, really good, then please stay and let me kiss you."

Her enigmatic smile is back, daring me to stay. Breathing

against her mouth, I glance to the door and back. It's warm in here and I can already feel beads of sweat forming on my skin. I have a feeling what is about to take place in this room won't be vanilla, but if I leave, I'll always wonder what would have happened if I'd turned down the opportunity to spend the night with the bold and mysterious Phantom in New Orleans. The Phantom who set my body on fire. She's got some kind of hold on me and she knows it. Unable to resist her, I tilt my head and lean in, welcoming her mouth.

Her hand cups my neck as our lips brush and I let out soft moans that grow louder when we part them. Her tongue meets mine and the kiss is heavenly, insistent and deep and when her other hand laces through my hair at the back of my head, she pulls me even closer, making me squirm in her grip. She's a really, really good kisser. I close my eyes and sink into her embrace, any doubt as to whether I should be doing this, fading. She's pushed a button that signals 'go' and leaving is not an option anymore; I couldn't stop if I wanted to. Her tongue claims my mouth like she's sucking the life out of me, making me weak in every limb and all I can think of is that I want more. *More, more, more.*

"Turn around," she says after pulling away, and I do. My thighs are resting against the high bedframe and anticipation builds inside me as she pulls at the satin tie of my tight corset, its loosening finally giving me the breathing space I need. I feel her fumbling with the complexity of its lacing, then sigh in relief when the garment falls to the floor. When I turn back around, she's holding the long tie in her hand.

"This will be useful." She studies me for any signs of apprehension, and I have no doubt there are many flashing before her eyes. The flinch that crosses my face, my chest rising as I hold my breath, the quiver in my voice as I speak.

"What are you going to do with that?"

"I'm going to bind you to one of the bedposts," the Phantom says. "But only if you want me to."

Again, I don't answer. She places the black tie on the bed, giving me time to make up my mind, then starts unbuttoning the tiny fabric-covered buttons at the front of my dress, one by one. With the eerie music drifting up from downstairs, the candlelight highlighting the portraits in the strange room, and the masks we're wearing, it feels like I'm participating in some kind of satanic ritual. The calm, systematic manner in which she undoes my gown unnerves me, but I make no effort to stop her.

Finally, my dress falls open and she slides it off my shoulders, taking in my lean, pale frame. Coming from New York, I'm a little envious of the Southerners and their deep tan, but she seems to appreciate what she sees and traces the lace edge of my black bra, then continues down over my belly, only stopping when she reaches my matching black thong.

I sense that the sight of me is making her feel heated, because she takes off her blazer and hangs it over a chair, then starts unbuttoning her own shirt, only stopping at her navel. She's wearing a black sports bra underneath her shirt, her full breasts making for a gorgeous sight, and I can see the edge of her black boxers behind the waistband of her slacks.

I reach out to unbutton them, and she lets me, stepping out of them as they fall to the floor. Marveling at her gorgeous body, I want to touch her, but she catches my hands again and holds them up against the bedpost while she presses her body into mine.

The sensation of our combined heat and her soft skin draws a moan from my lips, and I need her to take me, to release me from the hard throb in my clit that's screaming for attention.

The Phantom takes the tie from the bed and holds it up. "I'm going to tie you to the bedpost now. Is that okay?"

My pulse starts racing and I vaguely register myself giving in, raising my hands above my head against the bedpost.

She kisses me again while she carefully ties my wrists together. I know she's only doing this to distract me from what's happening, but I don't care. Her mouth is driving me wild and I kiss her back like I've never kissed anyone before; sucking her empty, stealing her energy while I give her mine. For a moment, I feel like I'm as one with this stranger whose face I haven't even seen, and I don't really understand how kissing someone can feel this good.

"Do you trust me?" she asks, stepping back.

I look her up and down, my pussy dripping wet from the kiss, and I nod. "Yes."

"Good. The safe word is 'black'. If you want me to stop, just say 'black'."

5

My arms are stretched above me, my legs quivering when I realize that I'm helpless and at her mercy. I don't know her and I'm in a strange house, the music downstairs now so loud that no one will hear me scream if I do. The fear that rushes through me is curiously arousing, and the desire pumping through my veins dampens my hesitation. Anyway, it's too late to change my mind now. I can't move, and although I know she will free me if I ask her to, I don't want to be untied.

I've never been in this situation before—bound and submissive—in the hands of a masked stranger, especially one revealing only half their face. "What are you going to do with me?"

She inches closer and kisses me softly, almost tenderly. Her cold hands move under my bra, finally skimming my breasts and it feels so good that I groan in pleasure. My nipples harden at the rush of her touch, and my breath becomes ragged and heavy. She lifts my bra and shakes her head as if she's not quite happy with the logistics. "I've changed my mind; that bra needs to come off." She smiles at me. "Don't you agree, Miss Black?"

My eyes widen as she walks over to her blazer, reaches into the pocket and takes out a small army knife. Reading my fear, she shakes her head as her gaze cruises my figure. "I'm not going to cut you, Miss Black. I'm just going to take this bra as a souvenir." She cuts through the straps, yanks it off and puts it in her pocket, along with her knife. "It's mine, now."

I let out the breath I've been holding, cursing myself for thinking she would actually hurt me, because, she doesn't seem like the sadistic type.

Staring at my small breasts, she licks her lips and traces the curves at the sides while she kisses me again, harder this time. I've been craving her mouth in the moments we've been parted and eagerly welcome her tongue and her deliciously soft lips. Her mouth moves to my neck and she pulls my head to the side by my hair, then drags her tongue over my skin. I know she can feel my vein pumping fast, throbbing as a mixture of fear and arousal sends me to greater heights.

She pushes her hips into mine and bites my neck, hard enough to hurt, but not quite hard enough for me to make her want to stop, because I love the sting it leaves and the sensation it evokes, shooting me into a state of full alert in a matter of seconds.

I had no idea I liked this level of play and I'm feeling a little confused as I cry out because it causes me to twitch and I know I'm very, very wet. "Please," I beg, pushing my hips forward. I need her to touch me there. "I need more."

At my imploring request, she suddenly stops and steps back, then glances around the room as if looking for something. "How about a little foreplay first?" she says, as if her relentless teasing isn't foreplay enough.

"How about you just fuck me?" I'm surprised at my own boldness and feel my cheeks flush hot pink.

"Not yet. Patience, Miss Black." Her gaze drops to her slacks on the floor and she picks them up and eases her belt out of the loops. The black belt is thin, made of supple leather, and from the looks of the big holes and cracks at the end, she's worn it a lot. "It's not hard," she says, trailing the leather across my cheek so I can feel its softness, and my heart rate shoots up—my mind now spinning—knowing scenarios I've only ever pictured in my fantasies, are about to become a reality.

She stretches it out and holds it up in both hands, then winds it around her right hand, holding it by the silver buckle. "Spread your legs, Miss Black."

When I don't immediately comply, she swats my outer thigh and I jump, more out of sheer shock than anything else. An even bigger shock is the fact that it turns me on. I never thought I'd let anyone spank me with a belt, let alone enjoy it, but here I am. A warm tingle is all I feel, apart from the initial sting, but the after-effects are sensational. The twitching between my legs won't stop, and I'm so sensitive that even the taut material of my panties seems too much against my pulsing center.

"Come on; that didn't hurt now, did it?" She smiles. "But the next one will, if you don't do as I say."

Slowly, I spread my legs apart, causing my body to lower, and my arms to stretch above my head. I'm trembling so badly that for a moment, I think she's worried about me.

"Black?"

"No." I shake my head and brace myself for the next lash —on the inside of my thigh—which is harder than the first but more anticipated, and I'm surprised at the moan that escapes my mouth.

"How does it feel?" the Phantom asks, whipping me once again in the same spot. "Describe it to me."

"It's..." I swallow hard and need a beat to catch my breath. "It's good. Stinging. A little painful but..." My voice is as unsteady as my legs as the end of the belt trails away.

"But?" She arches a brow and inches closer, bringing her mouth close to mine.

"But good painful, like all my nerves are exploding," I whisper. "I like it."

Her lips stretch into a smile against mine, but when I lean in to kiss her, she pulls back. "Somehow I knew you would."

Raising the belt, she whips me again, higher up and with force.

"Fuck!" I cry out as I writhe in my restraints—my natural instincts kicking in as my body twists to protect itself. The belt only just missed my pussy, and even though the thought of if landing right between my legs is agonizing, I still want her to move higher.

"Are you okay?"

"Yes, I'm okay," I say through heavy pants. Needing a break to compose myself, I contemplate using the safe word, then change my mind. It felt good, so why deny myself something I like? Emboldened, I say, "Do it again."

The Phantom hooks her fingers under the thin straps of my thong and pulls it down, leaving me even more vulnerable and exposed. I step out of them and with her feet, she spreads my legs apart again. "Beautiful."

My arms and legs are tired and sore, and using my last

strength to keep this position, I shut my eyes tight and wait for the blow. When the leather hits my oversensitive pussy hard, I groan loudly, not sure if I'm about to climax or burst into tears. It feels cold and warm at the same time, painful and incredibly good. I'm not sure if I can take anymore and as if sensing that, she drops her belt to the floor.

"I'm going to make you come now," she whispers. "I'm going to make you come harder than you ever have."

I take in a quick breath as she steps closer, and I'm dying to see her face even though it's much easier to flirt when wearing a mask, to go a little further while pretending to be someone you're not. I realize then that I've never been so impulsive as I've been with this stranger tonight. Our eye contact is electric, and it leaves me wanting more.

"Please take off your mask."

"No." She shakes her head and smiles. "You're here as my guest, so you follow my rules."

"I need to see you," I say, tilting my head to study her. She feels more powerful with her mask on; that much is clear. "I don't care what you look like," I continue, glancing at the covered mirror. "I just want to see your face."

She ignores my plea and lowers her hand between my legs, and I shudder at the delicious sensation of her feeling me up. Spreading my legs more, I welcome her fingers. I'm close, so close. She explores me, tracing my slick folds until I'm gasping and moaning, then she pushes two fingers inside me while she claims my mouth.

The combination of being filled up and kissed like this after she has stopped me from coming for so long, immediately sends a wave of warmth through my core. She withdraws, then enters me again and starts fucking me hard and fast while she kisses me, her mouth never leaving mine. I love the power she has over me, how she can make me explode while I'm at her mercy, and it doesn't take long before my guttural sounds are dampened by her lips. When I'm balancing on the edge, she curls her fingers, hitting a spot inside me that causes me to cry out.

My orgasm is earth-shattering, like nothing I've ever felt. She draws wave after wave out of me, and she doesn't stop until I have nothing left to give and my legs threaten to give way underneath me. My arms are stiff from being lashed to the bedpost, and she unties them, slowly lowering them while I groan at the ache in my shoulders.

She chuckles softly, and I'm only then aware that I'm staring at her like she's a ghost, because frankly no one has managed to make me feel this way before.

"Was that good?" She kisses me again while she strokes my pussy, and I'm pretty sure I could happily spend days tied up in this room with her.

"I think you know the answer to that question."

6

Falling onto my knees is all I can do, and even with the mask I can see she's surprised as she looks down at me. Without waiting for permission, I pull down her boxers and run my hands over her ass and her thighs as she steps out of them. Her muscles tense, and for a moment, I think she wants to stop me, but she makes no effort to deter me. Her demeanor seems calm, but I can tell by her quick breaths that she has a storm brewing inside and is in two minds about this as she ultimately wants to be in control. Finally, she leans back against the mattress, gripping the bedsheets as she waits for me to devour her with a dark look in her eyes.

I don't know how she does it, but this woman is driving me insane, bringing out a carnal side in me I didn't know I had. Leaning in, I kiss the soft hairs between her legs before I lower my mouth to taste her. She tastes so good, and I realize how much I've missed the taste of a woman as I run my tongue along her lips and over her throbbing clit. It makes her quiver, and her knuckles turn white as she clamps her fingers around the edge of the mattress.

"Fuck, yes!" Jerking her hips forward, she groans loudly, her eyes shut tight. I pull her in by her hips, wanting more of her, and melt into her body like fire on ice. Repeating my teasing actions, I draw another cry from her mouth and know she's already close. She's so wet, and her copious juices only fuel my hunger for her.

Closing my eyes, I let out a sigh of delight and take all of her, running my tongue up and down, inching inside of her just a little, before I move back up to suck her clit into my mouth. It pushes her over the edge, and I suck harder and bury my face in her pussy, wanting to give her as much pleasure as I can. She shivers as the feathers on my mask tickle her skin, and I can feel the sexual energy racing through her. Smiling at the sound of her pleasure that echoes through the room, I let her push me tighter into her as she laces her fingers through my hair. Somewhere in the back of my mind a little voice tells me I'm not myself right now, or maybe I'm exactly who I need to be because this feels amazing and there are no limits to how much I want her.

Bucking wildly against my mouth, she comes with a force that makes me moan loudly myself. Knowing I'm doing this to her makes me feel powerful and the sensation of her pulsating clit against my lips takes my breath away. However raw, this is incredibly beautiful too. The way she crumbles before me while she comes; weak and vulnerable, letting down her guard because she simply has no other choice than to let go.

"Fuck," she huskily whispers after her moans have finally faded out.

My hands relax around her thighs, and I'm thinking there's no doubt I've left marks there. Then, it's quiet again and there's only the steady thumping of the music downstairs.

I stand up and wipe my mouth with a smirk as I face her. Time is a blur and although it seems like we've been in this room forever, we haven't even gotten into bed yet. Her half-naked body is bewitching in the candlelight and noting that it's surreal to see someone in very little but a mask, I realize I must look the same to her. An anonymous body. No name, no face, just pleasure. But I'm curious, because despite the anonymity, I feel so much closer to her than I normally would to a stranger. I trust her. "Now can I see your face?"

She lets out a chuckle between short breaths, still coming down from her shattering orgasm. "No. Not yet. The fun is only just starting."

"Then will you at least tell me something about yourself, Ms. Phantom?" I ask as I ease the open shirt off her shoulders and pull at her sports bra to take it off.

She stands up and takes my hands, letting me know the power has shifted back to her again. "How about we wait until the sun comes up? Then I'll tell you everything you want to know and more."

"That sounds like something from a fairy tale, but I think I can live with that compromise." I get all heated when I see the fire in her eyes; she's clearly not done with me yet.

"That's a deal, then." My mysterious bedfellow smiles. "After all, it would be a waste not to make the most of our night..." She lifts me up, and I gasp at her unexpected demonstration of strength. With her hands on my behind, she steadies me onto her hips, and I wrap my legs around her waist, and my arms around her neck. It's incredibly sexy how she turns us around and drops me on the bed like I weigh nothing.

"God, you're strong," I say, shooting her a flirty smile. "Do you work out?"

"Half an hour, every day. But tonight, I'm planning on a

longer session because I especially like my equipment." Crawling over me, I know she's showing off, but I like that she wants to impress me.

"I don't mind being your equipment." I'm quiet as the heat rises between us again. My clit pulses from the feel of her naked belly against my sensitive flesh but the slow base in the background reminds me that Tessa might be worried or looking for me. I've completely forgotten about her and feel a stab of guilt as I glance at the door. I only arrived yesterday and already I've abandoned her for this woman I know nothing about. She seemed more than happy earlier, but she doesn't know where I am, and I want to make sure she's okay. "But I want to let Tessa know I'm here first."

"Okay. Are you sure you're ready to go downstairs?" The Phantom arches a brow as she traces the side of my waist and my hips. I'm not quite sure I understand what she means. "It might have gotten a little debauched by now," she clarifies. "It's past midnight and you might not be prepared for what you'll see. Want me to come with you?"

"After what you just did to me, I think I can handle anything," I say, searching for my dress. Eager to get back here as soon as possible, I don't bother with the corset, my shoes, or even my underwear. "I'll be right back."

7

The second floor, where the bedroom I've just left is situated, is empty of partygoers, but as I reach the first floor, my breath hitches as I see two women on the staircase. They're making out, and the blonde on top has her hand under the other woman's mini skirt. She's fucking her, and it's shocking to me as I'm not used to seeing anything like this, but at the same time, it's also incredibly sensual to voyeuristically watch them in their skimpy white dresses and masks, their lips locked and eyes closed as they let out soft murmurs of pleasure.

There's no other way to get downstairs but to walk past them, and I'm glad I have my mask to hide behind. Making sure to tiptoe, I hope they won't notice me, but as I pass them, one of the women grabs hold of my ankle. Holding onto the bannister, I steady myself, so I won't fall.

"Want to join us?" the blonde asks, looking up at me while she hikes up the other woman's dress, showing me that she's wearing nothing underneath. "She tastes divine." The words are spoken slow and low, almost like she's in some kind of trance, and she brings her finger to her lips and sucks it into her mouth.

I shake my head and try not to stare as she spreads the woman's legs and goes back to lapping at her clit. "No, thank you."

She doesn't pressure me, but she doesn't apologize either, and I wonder if this is normal to them. The answer to that question comes soon enough when I walk into the hallway, where more women are making out and pleasing each other—most of them naked— their moans mixing with the slow music. As I come closer, it sounds like they're humming in sync, and there's a strange sense of togetherness. The way their bodies move in slow-motion like they're all hypnotized, or equally intoxicated is fascinating. Nothing is rushed here, every second being enjoyed like it's their last.

I've never seen anything like this, and although I'm not sure what to do with myself, I allow myself to gaze over the crowd for a while. Hungry looks are being cast my way, an assortment of women silently inviting me to join them. It's sexy, and as I continue my search for Tessa heading into the big living room, my mouth falls open when I see everyone is naked in here too. Glistening, sweaty bodies glide over each other on the couches and the floor. It reminds me of a snakes' nest; dangerous but fascinating.

The sounds of pleasure and orgasms echo through the room, again, blending in with the music that seems to have been tailored for the event. Gasps, heavy breathing, sighs, the occasional climatic scream... Languid limbs are entangled in a slow and slippery dance, and the room smells of sex and incense. I notice I'm walking slower myself, and the word 'ritual' springs to mind as I wander between the entranced bodies. I've read about opium orgies in the early eighteen-hundreds and this scene certainly fits what I imagined them to look like.

"Tessa?" I whisper so as not to disturb the vibe when I spot her on a chair, still making out with Stephanie. They're both naked now and she's so into it that she doesn't hear me. It's not until I touch her glistening back that she turns around and looks up at me. This is so unlike Tessa that I can hardly believe she's doing this, and I want to make sure she hasn't been drugged.

"Hey, babe," she says, shooting me a lazy smile, as if her being naked on top of another woman while talking to me is nothing out of the ordinary. "Are you having a good time?"

"Yeah." I study her pupils to see if she might be under the influence of something other than alcohol, but there's no sign of it and she seems truly happy. "Are you okay?"

"Better than ever." She runs her hand through Stephanie's curls while she continues kissing her neck. "I'm going home with Steph, so don't wait for me. Unless you want to come too?"

The question makes my brows shoot up. Apparently, anything goes tonight. "No, thank you. You have fun, though." I smile back at her but have already lost her attention as her lips are on Stephanie's neck again, her hands slipping down to her breasts while Stephanie leans back and closes her eyes.

I stare at them for a moment, simply because it's hard not to, then turn my attention to the four women on the couch who are licking, stroking and fucking another woman who is moaning and writhing, completely oblivious of my presence.

On the floor are two brunettes, their bodies aligned and inverted, their mouths between each other's legs. The one on top is arching her back as a tongue darts inside her, and they're moving like one, taking their time as they buck their hips, their hands roaming over bare skin. No one has taken off their masks and I'm glad I'm wearing mine as I already feel like the odd one out in my dress.

When I'm about to leave, I spot a woman who's wearing a strap-on, sitting on a chaise longue by the window. Her hands are clutching the hips of a red-headed woman who's straddling her. She's slowly lowering herself onto the shaft, then raising herself while she throws her head back. Their lustful dance is incredibly erotic, and I can see that she's close from the way her body's trembling. The music speeds up in the most random way, and so does she. Rocking her body, she's basking in a state of euphoria that I've rarely witnessed, and it turns me on beyond belief. I want to leave and get back to the bedroom, but at the same time, I want to see her explode before I go.

Leaning against the door, I watch them from a respectable distance, my arousal growing as she climaxes with a loud moan. I'm shocked to see the woman with the strap-on has spotted me, and I'm even more taken aback when she waves me over to join them.

I shake my head and smile at her. Making a conscious decision to leave, I cast one more glance over my shoulder and see that someone else has crawled onto her lap, replacing the red-head, who is now lying on a rug on the floor, clutching her chest as if she's trying to catch her breath.

It's too much, and I run out knowing I'll get sucked in myself if I don't leave right this minute. I now understand Tessa's out-of-character behavior, because this party is toxic in the best of ways and I would have gotten swept away on this hedonistic wave, too, if I had stayed down here with her. As I walk up the staircase again, lost in my own thoughts, I realize nothing is normal about this night and I feel like I'm dreaming.

8

"That was interesting," I say when I return to the room and close the door behind me. Unlike before, the bedroom is a safe place to me now. The music is muffled but it still affects me, and I feel an immense hunger for more of her.

The Phantom's eyes gleam with devilry as she looks me up and down. "Do you want to go back downstairs?"

I think about it for a moment, because the sight of naked bodies and public sex has aroused me even more, if that was possible, and I feel like I'm in a trance-like state myself. "No. I'd rather stay here with you. Do you want to go downstairs?" My masked lover is lying in bed now, and from the looks of it, she's entirely naked. "You're already dressed for the occasion."

She laughs. "I'm more of a one-on-one kind of woman myself," she says. "But if I didn't have you here, I probably would. I'm not one to say no to anything that feels good."

I take off my dress while I walk over to the bed, then climb on, tear the bedsheets off her and straddle her. "How about I make you feel really good, then?" Finally, I see her full breasts and erect nipples, luring me in to fold my lips around them, and my hunger is fueled like never before, longing tugging at me.

Pushing me off her, she turns us around and covers me with her body. Her weight feels amazing and I spread my legs and close my eyes as she grinds into me, sucking at my neck. It's thrilling, euphoric, the shooting pain of her bites that follow almost sending me into an early climax. "What am I going to do with you?" she says in a husky voice.

"What are you going to do with me?" I repeat the question, dying to know the answer. I'm not even close to tired, and I intend to stay up all night, waiting for the moment she'll finally reveal a little bit about herself.

"I think I'm going to start by making you turn around and get on your hands and knees," she says with a mischievous smile, easing off me. Although she's smiling, I can see from her eyes that she's serious. "I might have slipped earlier because you're simply irresistible, but I'm still in charge tonight."

I do what she asks me and feel her nails scrape over my back. Her touch makes me jerk my hips back to meet hers, but she takes me by the waist and stops me.

"Stay still, and keep your eyes fixed on the wall. And the safe word is 'black', remember?" She moves my hands to the headboard and covers them with her own, then bends over me and adds, "I only want to give you pleasure, Miss Black. If it doesn't feel good, you need to tell me because I can't see your face like this."

I nod and comply, clinging onto the headboard as it's hard to keep myself upright with my legs quivering. It's like this woman can read my fantasies, and I'm ready for anything she's willing to give me.

"Stay there. Very still." Her voice has taken on another

tone altogether, colder and more businesslike with an undertone of amusement. This is a game to her and she's enjoying herself, but I'm yet to find out how I feel about this. "If you move your hands or look behind you, I'm going to punish you. Is that clear?"

"Yes," I mumble, my voice trembling with anticipation. Not knowing what's coming is excruciatingly hard, especially as she keeps still and doesn't say a word after this. I know she's there, but nothing is happening in the long moments that follow. It goes against all my instincts and without thinking, I glance over my shoulder. *Fuck.*

She arches a brow, her smile widening, and I immediately turn back but it's too late. A firm slap on my ass draws a gasp from my mouth and I flinch.

The sound of her flat hand hitting my skin is loud and harsh, but I love the sensation and the feeling it evokes. Another hard slap on the same spot makes me twitch, and I moan when she moves my knees apart. Knowing she can see how wet I am and how much I'm enjoying this arouses me like nothing else.

"You asked for it, Miss Black." She rubs the stinging skin, then runs her hand so low that she's almost between my legs. I wiggle and push back, craving more, but she repeats the action on my other cheek, much harder this time.

"Fuck!" Tears spring to my eyes, but it's more out of surprise than pain. The stinging of my skin feels warm and weirdly comforting, the glow spreading over my entire backside.

"Are you okay?" She pulls at my hair and pushes her hips against my ass.

"Mmm..." I feel her hand move between my legs and groan when she strokes my pussy. I can't seem to think or even process her question.

"Answer me, Miss Black."

"Yes, I'm okay," I say through heavy breaths, then make the entirely innocent mistake of looking over my shoulder again. It's just a habit; I like to look at people when I talk to them, but I'm punished with another hard slap, then a second, and a third.

"Aaaaah!" My loud drawn-out cry subsides into a moan, and I bite my lip so fiercely I almost make myself bleed.

"Still okay?"

"Yes," I say in a whisper. I'm not sure if she can hear me, so I clear my throat and repeat my answer. "Yes."

"Good." Her finger slips inside me, and I push back against her hand. When she adds another and continues to pull my hair, I'm close to exploding.

I don't know how she does this, but I'm a heaving mess with a one-track mind. All I want is for her to fuck me hard and fast and she does, slamming her hips into me with each thrust.

I let out a groan when she spanks my behind again, over and over, and she doesn't stop until I climax, moaning loudly as my walls clench around her fingers. Spasms, chills, stinging pain from the spanking and waves of orgasmic delight culminate into a ball of fire deep in my core.

Panting heavily, I crumple to the mattress as my knees give way, and she follows me, collapsing onto my back. Then she takes my hands and kisses my neck softly and tenderly while she lets out a deep sigh, seemingly just as relaxed as I am right now.

Her skin on mine feels heavenly, and I'm basking in a warm glow, my new state of ultimate comfort slowing my heart rate to the point where I can't even feel it beating anymore. I can still hear the music, but it feels strangely quiet. It's an internal sensation that I couldn't describe if I tried. "Who are you?" I ask again.

She rolls off me and I turn on my side to face her. I smile when our eyes meet and she smiles back, filling me with something that feels pretty close to happiness.

"Kiss me," she says, and I cup her face and press my lips against hers.

9

I have no idea what time it is when I tear myself away from her. We've been making out for so long that my lips are sore, and I'm clammy and feel like freshening up.

My paramour is a delightful surprise, and even though everything about this night has been totally out of my comfort zone, I don't regret coming here, because I've had the best sex in my life with an intriguing and gorgeous woman. She's still wearing her mask, but it doesn't bother me anymore. I'm sure she has her reasons and whatever is underneath it, I know I'll love, if I ever get to see her face. "Is that the bathroom?" I point to a door in the corner at the other end of the room.

"Yes, but it's currently out of order, so you'll have to use the one down the hall." She throws me the bedsheet. "Second door on the left. I don't think anyone will be up here, so if you don't want to use the sheet, well... by now you know no one will mind if they find you naked."

"Thanks." I wrap the sheet around me anyway because the thought of going out there naked is still daunting to me, even if everyone else is undressed.

The bathroom is spacious and quite stunning, but lacking anything personal. There aren't even toiletries by the sink, apart from a piece of soap and a small hand towel. I want to take my mask off to splash some water over my face but change my mind because it doesn't seem right to take if off anymore. Tonight, I'm someone else. I'm masquerading as someone who takes risks, someone who's not afraid to explore her sexual boundaries, and it's nice to be someone else once in a while.

My lips are plump and pink from endless hours of kissing, my hair a tangled mess, and when I inspect myself closer, I notice a small bruise on the side of my neck, from her teeth. The color is a deep red, surrounded by a blurry purple that is slowly spreading. I don't remember her biting me that hard; the pleasure I felt must have numbed the pain. My ass is sore from the slapping—I'm pretty sure she's left marks there too—but I love the warm glow on my skin and the memory of her hand landing on my behind over and over. Just thinking of it makes me shiver, and I find myself mildly conflicted. *What's come over me tonight? Why did I so willingly go along with her games? Why did I love it so much? And why do I want more, even now?*

Unable to answer those questions, I decide to stop overthinking things and wash my hands then wet the towel to cool my skin. My phantom has got me overheated and the cold cloth isn't helping one bit. My insatiable appetite for her is coming from deep inside and it seems that the more time we spend together, the more I crave her.

It's much quieter in the house now, and the music has been turned off. I suspect the party is almost over as I can hear people getting ready to leave in the hallway.

"Did you lock the door?" she asks as I throw the sheet back at her and join her on the bed.

"I think so, I..." I'm interrupted by the door opening behind me.

"Hey, what are you doing sneaking into this room?" I suppress a shriek as I look up to find the huge tree-sized security guard from earlier hovering in the doorway. She stares me down while I scramble for a pillow to cover myself with, then gasps as she spots my companion in the bed. Turning to her, her face pulls into a horrified grimace. "Seriously, boss?"

"Fuck..." Her eyes shift all over the place as if she's trying to come up with an excuse, but she's left speechless as she pulls the sheets up to her chin.

"Even for you, this is a new low," the security guard continues, shaking her head. "Sneaking into our client's bedroom? Bringing a stranger in here? You know very well the second floor is off-limits."

Now it's my turn to be shocked, and I stare at her, but she averts her gaze. "What's going on?" I ask. "Who are you? You're going to have to answer me now, because I don't like what's going on one bit."

"Fuck..." Apparently, that's all she's able to say now. "I'm so sorry, Miss Black. I'll explain everything outside. I think Daisy wants us to leave right away, so let's get dressed, okay?"

Daisy turns to face the door, giving us privacy to get dressed. It seems redundant, considering the house has been filled with naked women all night, but I still appreciate it. My second thought is that Daisy's sweet name totally contradicts her scary appearance and that Sequoia would have been more fitting. With her shaved head and huge biceps, she could very well pass for a cage fighter, and I don't intend to get on her wrong side. "So, are you going to explain what's happening here?" I'm feeling too irritated to wait for our talk as I put on my dress and stuff my underwear into my purse.

She's still avoiding my eyes as she slips into her slacks and buttons up her shirt. "Daisy works for me. I own the company that took care of the security here tonight." She hesitates, as if she needs time to think before she continues. "I was scanning the house before the party started and I saw this room. It was a little dusty and it clearly hadn't been used for a while since all the furniture was covered up in white sheets, so I knew no one would come in here. There's no reason for that sheet over the mirror; I just forgot to take it off. The key was in the door, and I borrowed it." She shrugs. "So I could use the room in case..."

"In case you got lucky? Oh my God, you're the worst." I let out a deep sigh, feeling foolish for falling for her lies.

Daisy seems as unimpressed as me, as she rolls her eyes while she turns back toward us. "Yeah, you are the worst."

"Do you even know Countess Montgomery?" I ask. "This is her house, right?"

Again, my phantom shrugs. "It is, but I don't really know her. Countess Montgomery is the best kept secret in New Orleans. She throws these lavish ladies' parties, but no one knows who she is—she must blend in with her guests or something, arrive with a formal invitation like everyone else."

I'm silent as I let the information sink in. "But she hired you, right?" I button up my dress and decide to continue barefoot as I can't bear the thought of putting my heels on again. With my corset and purse in one hand and my shoes in the other, 'walk of shame' is written all over me as I leave the room, passing Daisy who is holding the door open.

"Yes, she hired me over the phone, but I've never met her," she says as we descend down the stairs.

"She could sue you for doing this."

"I know. But I don't make a habit of bringing women into my clients' private quarters. It was just an opportunity too good to pass, and if you're happy to keep this between us..." The way she says it makes it sound like it's no big deal at all. "You and Tessa seemed harmless, and you especially kind of adorable. Daisy doesn't mind me sneaking girls into parties every now and then. I'm her boss after all, but I guess I went a little too far this time."

"You sure did," Daisy says. She's walking behind us, chaperoning us like we're a pair of teenagers who can't be left to their own devices.

I take a moment to process what she's just told me. It's not a horrible thing she's done; she just used one of the rooms and pretended to know the hostess, perhaps like everyone here tonight. Maybe I should cut her some slack because I've had an amazing night and she might be in enough trouble as it is.

As I look around the grand hallway one more time, the magic from before has vanished like it was never there. Cleaners are mopping the floors and security guards are ushering out people. The lights have been turned up brightly and I regret ever seeing this behind the scenes vibe as I'm desperate to hold onto the mystery of tonight. I rush after her and try not to look at the crew clearing out the last evidence of the party. She might have lied about knowing Countess Montgomery, but I know that our physical connection was real, and leaving without a proper goodbye is simply not an option.

I must see her face.

10

_____

J udging by the faint light it must be after six am, and it feels strange to venture outside, into the front yard. Three security guards are standing by the gates, making sure everyone leaves quietly so as not to disturb the neighbors.

"Well, I guess the night is over." She nonchalantly takes off her mask and turns to me when we're out on the street. After I begged her to show her face numerous times throughout the night, the way she removes it so easily and without hesitation is almost surreal. There's no announcement leading up to the grand reveal, no anticipation. She simply pulls it off and looks at me regretfully. "I'm really sorry I lied to you, but I didn't expect us to have such a connection. If I'd known..."

I silence her by placing a finger on her lips and marvel at her boyishly handsome face. I've seen her eyes and her mouth, but it's not until now—now that I can see all of her —that she makes sense to me. Her dark, curious eyes, long lashes, sharp eyebrows, high cheekbones, and a dimple in her left cheek that was previously covered by the mask make me smile, despite the situation.

"May I?" she asks, reaching out for my mask.

I shouldn't really give her the satisfaction of seeing me now, but it seems pointless to punish her, and honestly, I want it to come off too. "You may."

She removes it slowly, as if she's scared, and when the morning breeze caresses my face, I blink a couple of times, rubbing the sore skin that's been deprived of oxygen for the last eight hours.

Her eyes tell me she likes what she sees as she runs a hand over my face, and I touch hers in return. There's no more mystery, no candlelight and no music to heighten the suspense. If I were Cinderella, it would be midnight now and the spell would be broken. We're nothing more than two ordinary people leaving a party and just like that, the night is over.

The anonymous naked bodies from before are now dressed, some passing us without their masks, or hanging around, waiting for their cabs. It's hard to imagine that they were doing what they were doing only an hour ago, and as otherworldly as they seemed then, now they're simply fellow human beings with phones, voices and facial expressions. I should be angry at her for lying to me, but I'm not, too enticed by her face to think of anything else other than kissing her again.

"You're gorgeous," I whisper, then stop myself from saying something embarrassing because everything sounds way too real in the daylight.

"And you're hauntingly beautiful. Kind of what I imagined, only better." She gives me a small smile. "Are you staying far from here? My apartment is close by if you want to come back with me..." She pauses, lingering on the spot.

"Listen, I know you're angry with me and I know offering you a coffee isn't going to change that. What we just did… well, it requires trust, and I didn't want to tell you that I owned the security company because I knew that what I was doing was wrong. You must be disappointed, but if you'll give me the pleasure of making you breakfast, we can talk and maybe get to know each other a little?"

"You're right, I am a touch annoyed," I say. "You shouldn't have lied to me but it's not like you owed me anything and… well, I had a really good time." I swallow hard as my gaze lowers to her mouth. "Have you done this before?"

"Using my clients' private bedrooms to have sex with strangers? No. Crashing parties? Yes, I do that, sometimes." She shoots me a mischievous smile and it sends butterflies to my core. "I wasn't actually supposed to be here tonight; my girls were doing the work, so they'll lock up." She leans in closer and runs a hand through my hair. "I really am sorry."

My lips brush hers, and the touch is making every nerve in my body tingle with longing. Something so thrilling can't be so wrong, I think to myself as I part my lips to let her kiss me with a tenderness that wasn't there before. Now that I've seen her face, it's like I'm kissing someone new all over again. It feels different, even more intimate than before, and I pull her in and deepen the kiss as my fingers lace through her hair. It's wonderfully soft and thick now that the hair gel has dried, and I can feel her need through the tremble in her hands that are making their way down my back. We're getting carried away and need to stop; we're in the middle of the street and apart from the crowd leaving the party, a mailman is doing his round and people are walking their dogs. Desire is raging through me as I pull away and step back, staring at her while I run a finger over my lips. I know my brazen expression is giving away that I still want her very, very much, but I don't care.

"It's fine." I glance down at my bare feet. "We were just two strangers."

"We don't have to be strangers." She tilts her head and I'm trying to work out if she just wants me to come back to her place because she feels bad, or if she genuinely wants to spend time with me. There's more in her eyes than just regret, though. There's fire and passion of the deepest, darkest kind. Whatever the situation is now, what we shared was special and I know she felt that too. "Come home with me." Her hand snakes around my waist and it feels wonderful. I know I won't be able to resist her if I try, so I nod and let her lead me away.

"Okay. Take me to your place."

11

———————

Her spacious apartment is modern and tastefully decorated. Contrary to the bedroom in the mansion, I notice there is evidence of her living here. Brightly colored cushions are scattered over the couch and there are pictures of her and her family, I suspect, on the walls in her living room.

"In case you're wondering, this really is my place." An amused smile paints her lips as she joins me and hands me a mug with coffee. "I added a splash of half-and-half but there's more in the fridge, if you want."

"Thank you." I take a slow sip, savoring the taste of her excellent coffee.

"Those are my parents and my brother," she says before I get the chance to ask.

"Do they live around here?" I see that although she was much younger in this picture, she and her brother look totally different. Her brother has her father's strawberry blonde hair and she has her mother's dark features.

"They used to, but they died in a traffic accident twenty-nine years ago."

The statement throws me, and for a moment, I don't know what to say. "I'm sorry." I glance at her, but she avoids my gaze.

"Yeah, me too." She points to another picture. "That's me and Stephanie at our graduation ceremony. She's my family now; we've been like sisters since we were twelve, and she's the only person who knows everything about me."

"Did you ever date?" I ask.

"No, never. I had a crush on her when we were younger, but I'm not her type; she likes feminine women and besides, she's so vain that I wouldn't last a week with her." She chuckles. "And that's my team," she continues, glancing up at a large group photo. "They're not all female. I have twelve men and nine women in my employment but as you can imagine, a party like the one we attended last night required an all-female crew."

"You guys look close." The picture shows them sitting by a lake somewhere, holding up their beer bottles around a firepit.

"We are. New Orleans is the home to some extraordinary parties, so we're never short of things to talk about and we all know each other pretty well."

I take a sip of my coffee and look around the living room that has floor to ceiling windows overlooking the Mississippi River. It lays still with only a few boats cruising along while the sun rises, casting a warm glow over the water. It's a breathtaking sight, and I'm impressed by her view. "Now that the sun is up, are you finally going to tell me your name?"

"Kameron," she says, then adds, "With a 'K'."

"Kameron..." I repeat her name, letting go of simply thinking of her as 'the Phantom'. "It's nice. I guess it suits you, now that I know."

"It's Scottish." She hesitates as if she wants to elaborate, then shakes her head. "So now you know everything about me, it only seems fair you tell me your name and what you do for a living."

"My name is Ivy," I say. "Ivy Giacometti and I'm a night-club singer."

"A nightclub singer, huh? That's sexy. And an elegant name to match your alluring face. Are you Italian by any chance?"

"I am. My parents are both Italian, but I was born in New York. I still live there and the reason I'm here is to spend a few days with Tessa. She's my best friend and she moved here a while back."

"I'm glad you decided to visit." Kameron gives me a big smile and now that I can see her whole face, it's utterly charming. "Would you like to take a shower while I make us some breakfast?" She purses her lips. "Or we could have a shower together?"

"I think I'll vote for a joint shower," I say playfully as I inch closer, because the thought of being under the running water with her is simply too good to resist.

"Then we'd better get you out of that dress, Ivy." The sound of her saying my name turns me on and she knows it. "Ivy." She repeats my name and licks her lips. "I like it."

Slowly, she unbuttons the front buttons and eases me out of it. I thought the daylight might change the dynamics between us, but it hasn't. She's still got that look in her eyes that tells me I'm hers and only hers, at least for now.

I undress her too and admire her strong body as she walks ahead of me to the bathroom. Broad shoulders, muscular arms and thighs, full breasts and an ass to die for, tempt my senses and I let out a sigh of delight when I finally lean in against her under the running water.

My hands move slowly as I rub soap all over her, keen to explore every inch of her body now that I can finally see her clearly in the light, and she does the same to me.

Her breath hitches when I run my fingers over her nipples. They rise to attention under my touch and she bucks her hips against mine while she grabs my ass and pulls me closer. I'm so turned on by her that I have to force myself to go slow. My hands move to her hips, then trace the inside of her thighs. Just before I reach between her legs, she catches my hands and places them deftly behind my back with a teasing smile.

"You first." Kameron pushes me against the cold tiles of the shower wall. Holding my hands with one hand, she pumps soap into the other, leans into me and runs her fingers up and down my body. She rubs my breasts and the slippery sensation feels so good. Lowering her hand, she runs her fingers over my pussy and through my folds.

I gasp and throw my head back at the flash of delight it causes, writhing in her strong grip. My oversensitive pussy is pulsating, and her slow and lazy movements almost send me over the edge. "More," I beg through moans.

"More?" Kameron brings her lips to mine and kisses me while she rubs harder, then pulls away just as I'm about to come.

I'm clinging onto her because my legs won't hold me up anymore, and I'm panting and moaning against her shoulder.

"Spread your legs and I'll see what I can do." She takes the showerhead and turns up the pressure. Her eyes are twinkling with fire as she aims it against my pussy and sucks at my neck at the same time, sending me into euphoria.

I cry out, dig my nails into her back and clamp onto her while my climax courses through me. She doesn't stop until

I'm so sensitive that it hurts, and I have to beg her to take the showerhead away.

"Now do you still want more?" she asks, focusing her attention on me while she lets go of my hands and holds me up by my waist.

"No." I shake my head and laugh. "I seriously can't take any more." Trailing my fingers along her spine, my mouth is drawn to her neck and I kiss her just below her ear. The urge to please her in return is the only thing keeping me standing, her delicious naked body enticing me to do wicked things to her. Trailing my tongue over her earlobe, I lean further in to whisper in her ear. "But I have something else in mind."

12

Sitting on Kameron's street-facing balcony, I'm wearing nothing but one of her white shirts and my panties. There's a chill in the morning air, but the sun is warming my bare legs that are resting on her lap while we eat croissants and talk over more coffee. It feels surprisingly normal to be here with her, and I find myself entirely at ease in her company.

My body is in a state of blissful relaxation after what she did to me throughout the night and earlier in the shower. Tired and sore in all the right places, I shift in my seat and smile as I watch her spread jam over her croissant. I feel a little smug for finally having had sex again, and not just any kind of sex. The past ten hours were probably enough to get me through a whole year, but I have a feeling Kameron isn't shy of a one-night stand.

I tell her about my life in New York, and she tells me about her life here. I've learned that she loves her job, and that she started her security company after being in the army and working as a personal bodyguard for ten years.

"Did you ever get hurt?" I ask, trying to remember if I saw any scars.

"Nothing serious. A couple of broken ribs and a cut on my arm when someone attacked one of my clients in a bar, but that's it." Kameron rolls up the sleeve of her sweatshirt and shows me a faint scar. "I've been lucky I guess, but I knew I wasn't going to be lucky forever and I'm glad I decided to start working for myself. My last assignment was to protect this dodgy Russian guy and I didn't like how he treated his girlfriends. When I realized I'd rather kill him than protect him, I resigned and reported the asshole, so that was the end of my career in private protection." She shrugs. "My company is mainly hired by party organizers and sports clubs, so it's pretty straightforward."

"Does that mean you work at night a lot?"

"Yeah. I'm a night owl. And so are you, I assume, being a singer?"

"I guess you could say that." I take a bite of my croissant and lick my fingers. It was never meant to be sensual, but the way Kameron looks at me makes me think she would disagree. "I start around eight and usually finish around midnight. Unlike most professions, you can't sing for hours on end, so I do two or three sessions with breaks in between. If I'm with a band, we usually stay behind for a couple of drinks, so I tend to get home around two in the morning."

"That sounds like a fun life. Did you always want to be a singer?"

"No." I purse my lips and contemplate her question. "Well, I kind of wanted to, but I didn't think I could make a living from it. I was actually a PA before I started singing professionally. My band was my escape from my job which I didn't like at all, so one day I decided to see if I could make it work." I finish my coffee and lean back, enjoying Kameron's hands now rubbing my feet. "If I'd known it would be a hell of a lot more lucrative than a PA career, I'd have taken the leap years ago." I pause, a little surprised by how open I'm being with her as I'm normally quite a closed-off person. Social, yes. Personal, never. My sister always jokingly calls me a cold fish, as I'm the polar opposite to my other family members, who are an open book and take everything personally.

"I have a degree in modern art," I continue. "But I don't like teaching and I have little creative talent on that front, so apart from a couple of gallery jobs when I was younger, I never did anything with it. And now, I feel blessed doing what I love."

"You're an intriguing woman, Ivy." Kameron lifts my foot and kisses it. "So, what do you sing?"

"Jazz, blues... it depends on the venue. There are three venues where I sing weekly with a pianist, or a band, I have one monthly gig at a private members' club and then there are incidental bookings like weddings and such, which I don't love, but they pay well."

"I'd love to hear you sing," Kameron says, zoning out for a beat, as if she's imagining it.

"If you're ever in New York, let me know and I'll tell you where to find me."

"I certainly will."

Our eyes meet again, and the connection I feel is immense considering we only met last night. It throws me, so I change the subject. "Are you working today?"

"No. I have two days off. Do you need to go back to Tessa's place?"

"I'm sure Tessa is having a great time with your friend. She said she was going home with her, so I'm in no rush."

"Why am I not surprised she went home with Steph? My dear friend is a ladies' magnet."

"Her charms certainly worked with Tessa." I glance at my phone and I'm surprised to see that it's nine am. Not wanting to overstay my welcome, I get up and try to remember where I left my dress. "Well, I should probably let you go to bed."

Kameron stands up too and puts an arm around my waist. Her eyes meet mine, and she holds my gaze, making it impossible for me to resist her mouth. Even after hours and hours, I still haven't had enough of her, but as I lean in to kiss her, I bite back a yawn, only then realizing just how tired I am.

"If you have nothing to get back to this morning, stay here with me. I promise I'll let you sleep." Kameron shoots me a grin and shrugs. "Seriously, I'm tired too."

The idea of a comfortable bed rather than Tessa's couch sounds like heaven to me right now, and her offer seems genuine. "Are you sure you don't mind?"

"No, I'd love to have you here for as long as I can." Kameron takes my hand and leads me to her spacious bedroom, ignoring our cups and plates on the balcony. "Don't worry; the cleaner will do it when she comes in," she says when I make an effort to clear it up.

The bedroom floor is lined with a thick, cream carpet and it's decorated in neutral colors, modern and simple, like the rest of her apartment. There's a big bed next to floor-to-ceiling windows, again, with the same spectacular view over the river.

"God, that looks appealing," I say as I watch her draw the curtains and open the bedsheets for me to get in. I don't bother taking off my clothes, desperate to lie down. As soon as my head hits the pillow, my eyes start fluttering shut. Kameron gets in beside me and a warm glow settles over me as she wraps her arms around me. This feels perfect.

13

"Tessa?" I'm keeping my voice down as I tiptoe out onto the balcony to answer the incoming call.

"Oh, hey, Ivy. Are you home?" Tessa is whispering too, which tells me she's not alone either.

"No. Are you?"

"No." I know Tessa is smiling on the other side of the line; I can hear it in her smug voice. "I'm still at Stephanie's house. Are you still with the sexy Phantom?"

"Yes. She's still sleeping." I glance at the clock on the wall and see that it's three pm. "We didn't go to bed until this morning."

"We didn't either." Tessa chuckles. "I just thought I'd check on you, make sure she hadn't locked you up in a subterranean labyrinth beneath an old opera house."

"No, I'm fine. In fact, I'm more than fine."

"Good." Tessa pauses. "Well, if you're not home, I might go back to bed and have some more fun."

"You do that." I expect her to comment on what happened last night, and when she doesn't, I feel like I need to bring it up. Seeing Tessa naked with another women in front of dozens of others engaged in an orgy is not an everyday occurrence and it would be highly awkward not to talk about it. "But wait... what the hell happened last night?" I hesitate as I fiddle with a button on the white shirt I'm still wearing. "I came downstairs and everyone was naked and... well, you know..." I can hardly believe how prudish I sound after what I was up to myself.

"Hmm..." Tessa takes a moment and I can hear her taking a sip of what must be coffee. It stirs an urge in me to make some, so I go into the kitchen and wedge my phone between my ear and my shoulder while I try to figure out how Kameron's industrial machine works. "It was weird, right? I guess I got sucked into the atmosphere somehow. There was just this sensual vibe and it didn't seem that abnormal at all when everyone around me was doing the same. Even though it's entirely out of character for me, I don't regret it. In fact, I'd do it again. Where were you?"

"Upstairs, in a bedroom. Kameron—that's the Phantom's real name—said the hostess had given her permission to use it. Turns out, she's head of the security team that worked there last night and she lied about knowing her. We got busted; it was embarrassing. But it's fine, I'm over it."

"So you finally had sex?" Tessa sounds amused. "Good girl, it was about time."

I nod, even though Tessa can't see me. "I had more sex than I could handle. And she's cool, I really like her," I add while I put two cups under the machine. "Anyway, I'll see you tonight, so let's catch up then."

"Actually, would you mind if I didn't come home tonight? Just in case Steph asks me to stay. I know you came here to visit me, but I really like this girl and I think she might be the one." Tessa lets out a swoony sigh. "I wouldn't ask you if I wasn't totally head over heels about her."

I laugh at that because if it's up to Tessa, every single woman who crosses her path is 'the one'. "Of course not," I say. "It's not every night that you meet the woman of your dreams and even if she's not, it's a great opportunity to make a new friend." I'm secretly hoping Kameron isn't bored of me yet because the thought of crawling back into bed with her is making me wet. "I'll see you when I see you, then. I'm still here for four days so we'll have plenty of time to catch up before I leave." As I pour a little half-and-half into my coffee, I realize I don't know how Kameron drinks hers, so I take the carton and a pot of sugar into the bedroom. "Have fun, honey, I'll call you tomorrow."

Kameron is just waking up as I walk in and put the items on the nightstand next to her.

"Thank you. What a nice surprise that you're still here, I thought you'd left until I heard the coffee machine." As soon as I put my own cup down, she pulls me into bed with her and starts unbuttoning my shirt.

"You don't mind me still being here? I actually only woke up ten minutes ago."

"Not at all." Kameron shoots me a grin and opens my shirt, then traces her tongue over my nipples, making me moan. "But I've decided I want my shirt back," she jokes, then takes it off.

"Then what am I supposed to wear?" I ask innocently, moaning in delight when she rolls on top of me. Her naked-ness feels delicious and I wrap my arms around her, welcoming her body. She's so fucking hot, all sleepy and natural. No hair gel, no mask, and no front. It's just her, and she's perfect for me. Her full breasts are soft and her mouth persistent and greedy as she kisses me while she pushes her hips into mine.

"Nothing. Just the way I like it." She runs her hand

between my thighs, and I squirm when she traces my swollen lips. My pussy is so sensitive, and still sore from yesterday, yet I'm craving her fingers and need her now. "I can feel you want me and it's driving me wild," she mumbles against my mouth while her breath quickens. "Let me have you."

I move my legs apart and gasp as she enters me. There's no foreplay this time, no relentless teasing. She's not careful either, and I moan loudly as she starts fucking me. Her hips are pounding into me, her fingers moving deep inside me while she runs her thumb over my clit. I clench around her and close my eyes when her tongue claims my mouth with equal urgency and passion. She's taking me like I belong to her, like making me scream is her only goal.

"You feel so good," she murmurs as she pulls out of the kiss and looks down at me. "I think I'm going to keep you here so I can fuck you over and over and over..." Her voice trails away as my moans become louder, and I know she likes watching me while I explode. "I want you to come, Ivy."

Her dark eyes meet mine, and I tense up and let out a long, loud moan. There's so much fire in them, and when she feels my walls contract and my body shake, her lips part and she tilts her head, studying me. "Perfect," she whispers, as if she's feeling my orgasm herself.

I'm quivering with aftershocks and groan as she pulls out of me. She brings her fingers to her lips and sucks them in to her mouth. "Mmm... you taste delicious." The action is so sensual that I hold my breath and watch her as she does it again.

Biting my lip, I stare at her gorgeous face. Her dark features are captivating, her smile slays me, and it hits me then that I have a complete and utter crush on her. "I seem to recall you taste delicious too," I joke and turn us around, then roll on top of her. Kameron lets me, so I kiss her jawline and her neck, her breasts and her belly before working my way farther down. I'm craving her wetness on my tongue, and I'm rewarded when my lips meet a pool of it. She grabs hold of the back of my head, pushing my face between her legs.

"Fuck, Ivy!"

No one has ever screamed my name before, and it fills me with a sense of pride. Flicking my tongue over her clit, I make sure to drive her right to the edge, teasing her relentlessly before I make her come. She tenses and covers her face in her hands, as if she has no idea what to do with herself, and again, I hear the sweet sound of my name ringing through the room.

14

***

"Do you have a lot of girlfriends?" I ask as I'm lying in her arms, spent and relaxed after hours of raw and passionate sex.

Kameron arches a brow and looks at me. "Define girl-friends."

"I mean do you sleep around a lot?" I'm not sure why I'm torturing myself by asking a question I don't really want to know the answer to. In the very short time since I met her, I've realized I feel more comfortable with her than I've ever felt with anyone, and although I try not to overthink things, as I don't even live nearby, I can't help but wonder if this could ever be something more. Because that's all I want. More of her, more time together.

Taking a moment to ponder over her answer, Kameron twirls a lock of my dark hair around her fingers. "Honestly, yes," she finally says. "I have five or six girls in New Orleans that I meet up with regularly. I wouldn't call them girl-friends; I've always been clear that it's not going to be anything more than sex between us."

"Why not?" Frankly, I'm shocked by the 'five or six', but I try not to let it show.

"Because I believe that when you know, you know, and I've never felt anything other than arousal when I was with them. There wasn't that little extra something, a spark or insane attraction, I guess." She lets go of my hair and traces my cheeks and the gesture feels oddly intimate and sweet. "I don't let them stay over here. You're actually the first woman, apart from Stephanie, to set foot in my apartment."

"Really?" I frown, wondering why it was different for her with me, then scold myself for being hopeful. She probably just felt guilty for lying to me, and anyway, a daytime sleep-over doesn't really count.

"Yeah. I'm actually a very private person and not many people know me well. But it's nice to wake up with you, and honestly, I'd like to get to know you better." Her hand continues to caress my face. "Do you have women in your life?"

"No." I don't tell her that I haven't had sex in a year because that would make me sound like a total looser. I don't tell her that I've only been with four women in my life either, and that includes her. After Tessa, I had another girl-friend, then didn't date for years until I met my most recent ex. One-night stands have never appealed to me and I wonder why I was so easily persuaded last night. "And this is very unlike me."

"But you told me you were a nightclub singer. You must be super popular with the ladies. A hot woman with a great voice? Can't beat that."

"Everyone just assumes I'm straight," I say with a shrug. "So, it's mainly men who ask me out and I have no interest in men. I'm not very proactive in the dating department either, so that kind of limits my options."

"Ever been with a man?"

"Once. A long time ago, before I met Tessa. It wasn't for me. You?"

"Same." Kameron chuckles. "It definitely wasn't for me either." She turns on her side, resting her cheek in the palm of her hand as she leans on her elbow. "Do you like New York?"

"I do. It's my home and I feel at ease there. I live in Brooklyn and I love my neighborhood."

"Do you live in one of those cool brownstones?" Kameron asks. "Or is that just a cliché image that southerners have of cool people living in New York?"

"No, it's not a cliché and I do live in a brownstone apartment, actually. I bought it two years ago after saving up for ten years. It's so expensive there now."

"I bet. House prices have grown to enormous heights here, too. I bought this apartment seven years ago and already it's almost doubled in value." Kameron leans in and drags her tongue over my neck up to my ear. "Do you have a stage name? And what do you wear when you're performing?"

I laugh at the questions that just keep coming and shake my head. "I sing under my own name and what I wear... well, I guess you're going to have to see that for yourself. But it's my turn now, I want to know more about you." I hesitate for a moment, then ask the question that's been on my mind since last night. "The party... it was a little unconventional, to say the least. Do you go to parties like that often?"

Kameron seems amused by my question, and I have a feeling she likes my innocence. "There aren't many parties like that here, or anywhere for that matter. That's why..." She stops herself then, as if she's about to say something she shouldn't. "I guess that's why Countess Montgomery throws them four times a year. Because there's a need for them; they're always highly popular. My company has been doing the security for her since the very first party."

"So do you normally attend her parties yourself? When you're not working?"

"I might have a couple of drinks, but I don't participate in the fun, seeing as I'm usually working, and my staff is there. I took you to the room because I didn't want them to see me like that. Figured a little privacy would make me a very happy woman and turns out I was right. It was worth it, even though we got busted," she adds while her unrelenting stare lingers on me.

"What exactly happened?" I ask, wanting to know more. "It was like everything was happening in slow motion, like the guests were in some kind of trance downstairs."

"There's no magic involved, or witchcraft, if that's what you're hinting at. It's the combination of the right music, the lighting, and the anonymity and the mystery of the masks. The cocktails contained traces of maca, a Peruvian plant that enhances the libido, and concentrated wild lettuce, which can have a very mild hallucinatory and calming effect. They're both entirely harmless, natural and legal. The password was 'maca' by the way, so those who were invited knew exactly what was going on and you... Well, I did warn you." She winks. "But I don't think it was the maca that made you come four times."

"No, it certainly wasn't that," I say, a blush creeping onto my cheeks. "Do you make a habit of tying women up?"

"Now who's asking all the questions?" Kameron grabs my wrists and holds them above my head, then folds her lips around my nipple, sucking it hard into her mouth. I let out a groan of pleasure, squirming underneath her. She's strong, and the fact that she's holding me down only heightens my arousal. "See?" she says. "You like it, and somehow, I knew you would."

"I do." As she does it again, I let out another cry of pleasure. "But you still haven't answered my question."

"Sorry. Your nipples are so distracting that I forgot what you asked," Kameron jokes, letting go of me again. "But yes, I do tie women up occasionally. For their own pleasure and for my own. Aside from that it turns me on, it seemed fitting last night, with that big four-poster bed, don't you agree?"

"Yeah." I shiver as I think back to how she fucked me while I was tied up. How she spanked me until my cheeks were glowing red. "I think you're a little more sexually open than me," I say, after carefully considering my words.

"Is that a problem?"

"No." I blush even harder. "I'm curious. Perhaps I'd like to know more." I can't believe I just said that, but I did.

"You'd like to know more, huh?" A twinkle appears in Kameron's eyes. "How much time do we have?"

A flutter runs through me at her words. "I'm leaving Thursday morning." Loving this conversation, I wiggle in her grip, my pussy throbbing when I can't seem to free myself. The thought of more time with her and exploring a new world is making me heated and a little crazy, but the good kind of crazy.

Kameron looks down at me and tightens her grip. "Then let me take you out for dinner before we get started. I'm hungry and I'm sure you are, too."

15

"Hey there. It's Ivy, right? Tessa asked me to give you this." Stephanie hands me a bag after letting herself in and shoots me a bemused look as she points at the white shirt I'm wearing. "I'm sure you'll be happy to get into something other than Kameron's work shirt."

"Thank you." I give her a smile and open the bag, relieved to find lingerie in there, too. Stephanie looks so different from last night, dressed in a cute knee-length pink dress and a cashmere cardigan, that I barely recognized her. "That's so kind of you." I'm glad Tessa didn't give her my whole suitcase as I don't want Kameron to think I've decided to move my stuff here, but I do really need something to wear if we're going out for dinner.

"No problem and don't worry, I won't stay long; I know you guys are going out and I've got a cute girl waiting for me, too." Steph turns to Kameron. "And this is for you, babe." She holds up a discreet looking bag and Kameron eagerly takes it.

"Thank you." She turns to me and holds it up. "I asked

her to get me some stuff from a special store on her way here."

"What kind of stuff?" I ask, then feel myself blush when I see the logo and realize it's from a sex shop. "Oh…" Knowing how naïve I must sound, I quickly laugh it off and shake my head. "Never mind."

Kameron and Stephanie are grinning at me, and it's clear to me then how close they are if Kameron asks her to pick up sex toys for her. It wouldn't in a million years occur to me to ask Tessa to do that. Not that I use sex toys; I've never even owned one.

"We have no secrets between us," Stephanie says. "But don't worry; there's nothing physical going on here." She waves a finger between herself and Kameron. "Gross."

"Hey, that's kind of insulting," Kameron jokes, then turns her attention back to the bag. "Want to see what's in here?" she asks me.

"No. I kind of like surprises." That's a flat-out lie; I hate surprises and of course I want to know, but I don't want them to see my reaction when I pull out whatever's hiding in there. I probably won't even know what half of it is.

"Well, let me tell you, you're in for a treat, girl." Stephanie winks at Kameron. "You said all woman were suckers for a good strap-on, didn't you?" She blinks innocently when Kameron shoots her a warning look in an attempt to get her to stop talking. "What? That's what you told me when we were having cocktails last week."

"Seriously, Steph?" Kameron rolls her eyes. "Do you really have to say everything out loud?"

"Yes," Stephanie says matter-of-factly. "My mom always says, 'Let it all out because the truth is in the eye of the Lord'."

"Right. Well, I'm sure the Lord wouldn't mind if you kept

your thoughts to yourself now and then." Kameron looks a little uncomfortable, and I shrug casually to put her at ease, even though the mention of a strap-on has gotten me a little hot under the collar. Stephanie seems funny, and I get the vibe that they really are like family, which includes annoying and teasing each other.

"So, have you guys been having fun?" Stephanie asks, and I suspect she knows exactly what we've been up to.

"I've had enough fun to last me a lifetime," I shoot back. "How's Tessa?"

"Mmm..." Stephanie arches a brow and runs a hand through her curls. "Your friend is absolutely delicious and in good hands with me," she jokes. "I drove her home so she could get dressed and I'm going back there now because we're going for dinner, too."

"Why don't you two come with us?" I suggest without thinking it through. I turn to Kameron and wave a hand. "I'm sorry, I should have asked you first... Would you mind if they came along?"

"No, of course not." By the looks of it, Kameron isn't sold on the idea, but she doesn't say as much as she turns to Stephanie. "But I'm taking Ivy to *Madame Perle* and you don't like the food there."

"Nonsense. I love, love, love her food and I'm sure Tessa will, too." Stephanie claps her hands in excitement. "A double date with my bestie. This is a first, right?" She hesitates, then shakes her head. "No, wait. We had a double date with those twins we met in that hotel bar a couple of years ago, remember? The hot Scandinavian twins with the big..." She uses her hands to make a curving gesture in front of her chest.

"Yes, I remember, and this is not an appropriate time or

place to reminisce about past dates," Kameron interrupts her with a chuckle.

"You're right. Sorry about that, me and my big mouth…" Stephanie gives us a wave as she turns to leave. It's not just her appearance; her whole demeanor seems different from last night, I realize, as I watch her walk off. Weirdly enough, she reminds me of Tessa in a way. She seems just as impulsive and loud, and now I have trouble imagining them together because the idea is just too funny.

"Well, I'd better go before I make you look even worse, girlfriend," she shouts at Kameron before she heads out of the door. "We'll see you both later!"

Kameron lets out a long sigh of frustration and covers her face in her hands when we're alone again. "If you haven't gone off me yet, I promise you that you will after two hours with her."

"Is that so? Have you used that strategy before with women? Because it will take a lot for me to go off you and even after experiencing Stephanie's talent in that department, I doubt she'll succeed." I wrap my arms around her waist and shoot her a grin. "But I must admit, she's hugely amusing, and I can't wait to hear what else she has to say about you."

16

"Well, this is kind of weird." I sit down next to Kameron and look at Tessa. "Weird but fun." The small, dark restaurant is crowded, and the tables are placed close together. On a stage in the back, a band is setting up for the night, their quiet soundchecks and squeaking microphones a familiar ritual to me.

"On a double date with your ex, you mean?" Stephanie asks. "Tessa told me you guys used to date."

"No, I mean just a double date in general, it's my first time. I don't really see Tessa as my ex anymore. It was a really long time ago and now she's just my best friend, so we don't think of each other like that."

"It's been a long time for me, that's for sure," Kameron says. "I haven't been on a double date since I was in my twenties. Apart from the one with the twins Steph mentioned earlier of course," she corrects herself, getting back at Stephanie.

It's entertaining to observe their back-and-forth banter, and especially to see Stephanie blush now, as she glances at Tessa. It dawns on me then that I haven't asked Kameron about her age, so I turn to her and study her face. She has fine lines around her eyes but living in a sunny place, that's only to be expected, and with her being so athletic, age can be misleading. "How old are you?" I ask.

"I'm forty-seven."

"Okay." I look at Stephanie. "And then so are you, if you went to school together."

"Uh-huh." Stephanie nods, then frowns as she looks from Kameron to me and back. "Are you telling me you haven't even exchanged basic information like your age?"

I shrug. "It didn't seem important." The corners of my mouth pull up into a smile as I lean into Kameron and brush her shoulder. "Besides, we were kind of busy with other things."

"Yeah, we've been very busy," Kameron agrees, and places a hand on my thigh under the table. It immediately flares up my desire for her and it's a welcome reminder that we'll have a whole night to ourselves when we get back. *A whole night with whatever was in that bag.* "So, what about you?" she asks me. "I'm guessing you must be quite a bit younger than me."

"Thirty-five."

"Okay." From her reaction, she doesn't seem to think our age difference is a problem but then again, this is just a bit of fun, so who really cares?

I kind of like that she's older. I've never dated someone significantly older than me, and it's refreshing to spend time in the company of a woman who knows who she is, what she wants and where she stands in life for a change.

"Okay?" Stephanie looks at Kameron incredulously. "You find out you've bagged yourself a toy girl and that's all you've got to say?" I know she's joking and Kameron just laughs it off.

"What do you want me to say? Now that you've made a point of it, anything I say will sound ageist or inappropriate."

"True." Stephanie shrugs. "Anyway, let's show these youngsters what we're made of." She calls over a waiter and orders a bottle of bourbon and a bucket of ice. "Now, what are we having to eat? Do they have salads? I just remembered I don't really like the food here."

"Kameron is a total charmer, always has been. She's got ladies swarming around her anywhere she goes," Stephanie says after a couple of drinks. She's getting rowdier with every shot of bourbon but she's actually super entertaining. I can see Tessa is totally in awe of her. The way she looks at her and swoons over anything she says is endearing, and they seem to get excited about the same things, like shopping and facials, and some singer whose name I've never heard. I just hope she won't break her heart because Tessa is clearly already invested, but only time will tell.

"Come on, Steph. Not now," Kameron begs.

The night has been fun so far, and conversation is flowing effortlessly as we're sharing a fruit platter for dessert. I'm making sure not to drink too much, keeping in mind that we have plans for later, and I've noticed Kameron is doing the same. That thought keeps me rather restless, and I keep shifting in my chair, edgy and aroused.

Stephanie chuckles and points at Kameron's phone. It's on silent, but it's been ringing for a while now, and although Kameron hasn't noticed it, I have. I must admit, the timing is perfect after what Stephanie just said, and it's making me giggle, too. "Blonde girl with Chihuahua," Steph slams her hand on the table and cracks up as she reads out the caller ID. "You don't even remember her name, do you?"

Kameron seems highly uncomfortable with the situation. Although she laughs along, there's a hint of annoyance in her expression as she switches off her phone and puts it in her blazer pocket. "Seriously. Enough, Steph." She shoots me an apologetic look. "I'm sorry."

"Don't worry about it." I smile back at her, letting her know it's okay. This is only confirming what I already knew: Kameron is not relationship material, and this is nothing more than a fun fling. Soon it will come to an end and I will just be another forgotten name in her phone, so I might as well enjoy it while it lasts. I will go back to my single but happy life in New York, and she will most likely continue to serial date and fuck her way through the city. It is what it is, and I can live with that.

"So what about Stephanie?" Tessa asks. "Tell me something embarrassing about her. It's only fair you get back at her."

"Nah-ah." Stephanie waves an inebriated finger while she takes a long drink. "Don't get her started."

"I think Tessa has a point," Kameron says. "Let me think..." She pretends to be in deep thought, but I'm pretty sure she already has an arsenal of stories lined up.

At that moment, my phone rings, and when I ignore it, my mother sends me a message. *'I'm calling the police!'* I'm shocked to see that I already have over a dozen messages from her, and I quickly scroll through them.

"Excuse me, I have to make a phone call." I get up and sigh at the unnecessary drama my mother is causing. She's been trying to get hold of me, but I've been too distracted to check my phone and now she's alerted the whole family. It's not the first time this has happened, and although I've tried to explain to her multiple times that I have a life and that it does not necessarily mean I'm dead if I don't respond to her calls immediately, she clearly didn't get the message.

"There you are. Thank the good Lord!" My mother sounds terribly dramatic. "Why haven't you called me back? I've tried you fifteen times over the past few days so I had to ask your brother to break into your apartment after he unsuccessfully rang the bell at least three different times today. We've been worried about you. Where are you?"

"Sorry, I've been busy. I'm in New Orleans, visiting Tessa."

"You should have told me, then I wouldn't have called your neighbors and sent Eddie over."

"You seriously need to calm down, Mom. It's only been thirty-six hours since we last spoke. I called you before I left. And you had Eddie break my lock? Really?"

"Don't worry, he put a new one on and both your neighbor and I have a spare key now." My mother clears her throat. "Why didn't you tell me you were visiting Tessa?"

"I was going to tell you." I roll my eyes and groan. "But you just kept talking and talking about Eddie's broken van and this soap opera you've been watching and one of your customers who had a wart on her eyelid and God knows what else, and then I forgot."

"Okay. I understand and I accept your apology."

"Right..." Although I don't recall apologizing, I don't comment.

"And by the way," she continues, "it wasn't one of my customers who had the wart, it was your Aunt Lucia. Maybe you should give her a ring, she's having it removed on Friday and she's a little anxious about it. But more importantly, Sandra, my Friday regular who always comes in for a wash and blowout—she doesn't have any warts, at least not as far as I'm aware—is getting a divorce and I was thinking I should set her up with..."

"Mom, I don't have time for this now, but I promise you I'll call you when I get home, okay? And then you can tell me about all the warts and blowouts in the world. Now please stop worrying about me, I'm fine."

"All right, then." Just as I'm about to hang up, she manages to squeeze in another question. "Wait, who are you with?"

"Just Tessa and a couple of her friends."

"Friends? Someone you like?"

Damn it. She always knows when I'm lying; she claims my voice goes up a notch and I suppose it does. "Yes, they're very nice but I'm going to go now. Bye, Mom." I hang up before she has the chance to reply and make my way back inside.

"Anything serious?" Tessa asks with a worried expression.

"No, just my mom."

Tessa laughs and shakes her head. "Enough said."

17

"So, Ivy, what turns you on?" Kameron asks as we're walking back home. It's late but just like New York, this city never seems to sleep. The streets are crowded, and people are smoking and drinking in front of the overflowing bars, many hosting live bands or karaoke nights. It's like there's an energy here that I've not felt anywhere else, but I might just be getting carried away by the whirlwind inside me; Kameron has a way of stirring things up.

Dinner has been lovely and for the first time, we've kept our hands mostly to ourselves. Of course, there was flirtation. There was a lot of it, because it seemed impossible not to flirt, but I'm seeing a different side to her now. A very down-to-earth and human side, and I like it.

"What turns me on? Are we really going to have this conversation out here?" I ask, then look around to make sure no one is listening in. We're fine; people are minding their own business, and besides, there's too much background noise for anyone to listen in.

"Why not? It's nothing to be ashamed of." The way Kameron says it makes it sound like she is totally comfortable discussing her sex life in public. "Just tell me what turns you on." Her hand is resting on my back and she lowers it until it is pressing into my behind.

"Okay, I'll tell you." My eyes meet hers and an amused smile paints my lips as I note the desire in her gaze. I love that she wants me all the time. "But only if you tell me first."

"Fine. But I think you already know." Kameron grins. "I like to be in charge, and I like to please. Pleasing women in whatever way gives me a kick. In my opinion, there's no sweeter sound than that of a woman having a great orgasm and nothing tastes better than pussy." She squeezes my ass and pulls me closer. "And yours tastes exquisite."

I laugh it off in an attempt to hide how much this arouses me and put an arm around her in return. "Is that so?"

"Mmhmm." She leans in and lowers her voice while she brushes her lips against my ear. "But I like to fuck, too and as you now know, thanks to Steph, I have a brand-new strap-on at home. I might wear it for you soon."

I feel my cheeks turn pink as a flash of heat shoots between my legs. She's making me squirm and we're not even home yet. "I would love for you to wear it. I've never been fucked with one before."

"You haven't?" Kameron stares at me as if she can't believe what she's hearing. "Well in that case, my sweet, innocent Ivy. I can't wait to be your first." She twirls a strand of my hair around her finger "If you really want to indulge me, then let me tie you up and have my way with you. All night. I promise you won't regret it."

A heated glance passes between us and my body reacts in astonishing ways. The stirring, the buzz, the tingle that reaches every nerve. The rush of blood through my veins, causing throbbing and blushing and a wave of adrenaline.

My shallow breaths must give away that I'm down with whatever plans she has tonight, but that's not enough for her. She wants to hear me say it.

"Your turn." She pulls me into an alleyway and pushes me against the wall, grinding herself up against me while she runs her mouth down my neck.

"You've made me curious on many levels," I say. "I want you to show me, surprise me, have me. And I want you to know that I trust you with my body." I tilt my head and regard her. "Just don't forget my name, okay? I don't want to be in your phone as 'Miss Black', or 'Singer from New York'. Actually..." I add, changing my mind. "I'm okay with being *your* Miss Black, but only in bed, not in your memory. I want you to remember me as Ivy." Immediately I regret saying it, because it's broken the sexual tension between us.

Kameron freezes and a serious frown settles between her brows. "Ivy, you could never be just 'sexy singer from New York', or 'Miss Black', or 'hot Italian', although you are all of those things. It's different with you."

"Is it?" I don't mean to sound skeptical, but I do.

"Yes, it's totally different. I've never spent this much time with any woman, but the moment I met you I just wanted to be near you. And I'm not sure what it is, but you seem to have put this spell on me and that fascinates me; I don't even recognize myself like this."

I don't believe her, so I say nothing. The flattery rolls off her tongue so smoothly that I bet she says that to all the women she sleeps with. But it doesn't matter. It's all good, as long as she remembers my name.

"When I said I'd like to visit you in New York and hear you sing," Kameron continues, "I meant it."

Again, I remain silent and close my eyes as she brushes her lips against mine. Seeing her again once I go back home seems too good to be true and I don't want to get my hopes up. "Let's just stick with tonight for now."

"Okay." A hint of disappointment flashes across her features, but she swiftly composes herself and brings her hand down to caress my behind once more. "Then I'll just have to make sure that tonight is really, really memorable."

18

The bedroom is dark, and I'm lying on the bed, on top of the covers. My naked body is highlighted by a row of candles on the dressing table, and the large mirror behind them reflects the light, making the ceiling flicker as I look up. I'm trembling, unsure of what's coming, and the torture of anticipation has my mind spinning. After our conversation on the way home, I'm eager to find out.

Kameron gets on the bed and holds up two velvet covered cuffs, linked by a metal chain. "Give me your hands." Her voice is soft and sweet, and I don't think twice about lifting my arms above my head. Already turned on by the fact that she's straddling me, it dawns on me that I want this as much as she does. The swell of her breasts suspended above me is incredibly arousing and as she takes my wrists, I wish I'd run my hands over them while I had the chance.

She hooks the chain through a spike in the bedframe and fastens the cuffs tight enough to limit my movements, but they're comfortable and don't feel like they're restricting my blood flow. "Does that feel okay?" The fire in her eyes flares up at seeing me like this. It's the same look she gave me at the mansion, and I'm both nervous and dripping wet.

"I'm not sure how it's supposed to feel, but I'm okay," I say.

"Good." Kameron gets off the bed and steps back to look at me. She reminds me of a kid in a candy store and I think what she likes most is that everything is a first for me. The uncertain look in my eyes, and my fear, perhaps? She picks up the bag Stephanie delivered earlier and pulls out a fine chain with small rubber clamps at the end. Turning to me, she holds them up. "I have a pair here, but I wanted some that were a little gentler, for you. Have you ever tried these?"

"No. I've never tried anything before." As I say it out loud, I wonder why because all of this is thrilling. I swallow hard as I watch her bend over me with what I assume are nipple clamps. "Will they hurt?" I try not to think of all the other women she's undoubtedly used them on before, because tonight is just for us.

"A little. But I'll make sure it's the good kind of pain." Kameron bends over me and brings her mouth so close to mine that I can feel her breath. "I've loosened the tension. You decide if you like it and tell me if you want me to remove them."

Lifting my upper body, I try to kiss her, but she inches back, licks her lips and rakes her eyes over me. "You're so fucking beautiful," she says softly, before running a hand through my hair.

I move my head and lean into her touch, craving her warm skin. It brings me comfort, now that I'm trying something new. Fear ripples through me when she attaches one of the clamps to my right nipple. When she fastens it and lets go, I flinch at the intense ongoing sensation of pressure that makes my clit twitch. "Fuck…"

"Too much?" Kameron asks.

I take a moment before I answer, noting that the initial sting is settling into a dull and delicious ache. "No, I'm good." Taking a couple of deep breaths, I nod, giving her permission to attach the other.

Although she's in control, nothing will happen without my permission, and I'm learning that the ultimate power is with me. I decide how far I will go, and I'm ready to explore my boundaries.

My chest shoots up as she attaches the other clamp on my left nipple and again, I wait for the sting to subside. "It feels..." I'm not sure how to describe the feeling, because it's simply different from anything I've felt, but the combination of having my hands restrained and the pressure of the clamps on my sensitive buds is causing wetness to pool between my legs.

Kameron shoots me a smile and gives the delicate chain hanging between them a tug. She doesn't pull hard, but it's intense and makes me gasp. "Feels good, right?"

"It does," I admit, still panting from the shock.

"Have you ever worn a blindfold before?"

"No..."

"My God, you are innocent." Kameron leans in and sucks my bottom lip into her mouth, then bites it until I groan. "I like that." Again, she moves off the bed returning with a black, satin blindfold. "Lift your head."

I do as she says and when she puts it on, my pulse starts racing even faster. This is scary enough as it is, but now that I can't see what's going on, I'm feeling helpless and completely at her mercy.

Kameron strokes my cheek and kisses my forehead. I appreciate her attempt to put me at ease but by now, I'm a ball of tension, both turned on beyond comprehension and terrified of what's coming. "What are you going to do to me?"

"Our safe word is 'black', remember?" Kameron says, ignoring my question. "I promise I won't hurt you. I'm only going to make you feel really, really good." She tugs at my clamps again and the action is so unexpected—now that I can't see what's going on—that I let out a loud cry. Every touch feels so much more intense, and my nipples are so sensitive that I get a constant rush of sexual pleasure from the tightness.

As I lie there, the minutes that follow seem like hours. I hear her leave the room and come back with something clinking against glass and I quiver, not knowing what it is.

"Are you comfortable?" she asks in a husky voice.

I almost laugh at that, because this is quite possibly the most uncomfortable thing I've ever done, but I know she's referring to my restraints. "Yes."

"Excellent." I feel her climb onto the bed, and she takes one of my ankles and moves it aside, then gets in between my legs and moves the other one too, spreading me open.

I'm aware of my dripping wet pussy and my swollen clit, and I know she can see how aroused I am. I feel exposed and vulnerable, but I'm also on fire.

"Let's explore some sensations, shall we?" There's the clinking sound again, and I tremble as I wait. And wait. And wait. Nothing is happening but I know this is her way of heightening my desire—my sense of anticipation—and it's certainly working.

Then it happens. She runs something over my pussy and in a reflex, my hips shoot up. I have no idea whether the sensation feels extremely hot or extremely cold at first, my perception confused by the lack of sight and my body too tense to work it out. When the object starts dripping over my folds, I realize it's cold, and that it must be an ice cube. My heated sex is melting it and when she moves it up to my clit, I groan at the agonizing tingle it causes on the most sensitive part of my body. My arms tug at the restraints and when I realize I can't protect myself from her devilish game, a mild sense of panic settles over me. Using the safe word springs to mind, but I refrain from voicing it, not really wanting her to stop.

"Too much?" she asks.

I don't know how to answer that question. Yes, it's too much, but it also feels thrilling. When it gets so cold that it's almost unbearable, she removes the cube and I feel her breath between my legs, just before she puts her warm tongue on me.

"Fuck!" I cry out again, and she spreads my legs wider so that she can take all of me into her mouth. "Fuck, fuck, fuck!" It feels so amazing that I have trouble keeping still, but she holds me down with her strong hands and all I can do is surrender. My moans become louder and I'm so close, so ready to fall over the edge all of a sudden.

Then, she pulls away and there is nothing. "Not yet," she says in a teasing tone. "Not until I give you permission to come."

I groan in frustration, then cry out again when the cold hits me once more. She draws it out this time, keeping the ice cube there until it hurts, then swoops back down to repeat her incredible tongue action. I have no idea what she's doing but I never want her to stop.

My nipples are becoming numb, and my pussy is so sensitive that I think I might lose it if she doesn't release me. Finally, she says the words.

"Let go, Ivy." She swiftly removes the clamps and the sensation of blood flowing back into my nipples sends me to a heightened state of awareness, that and the fact she is now back between my legs sucking my clit into her mouth.

I scream, all my inhibitions shattering, and I let go like I've never let go before. The stinging pain on my breasts turns into a sensational glow, spreading out across my skin. It goes everywhere, even to the tips of my fingers and my toes. My pussy is throbbing against her mouth so hard that I know she can feel it. The rush is mind-blowing, and when she moves up and covers me with her body, I feel like laughing and crying at the same time. Something wet runs down the side of my face, and I don't even realize it's a tear until she wipes it away, then places soft kisses on my damp temple.

Sweat has pearled on my skin, and the cool breeze coming from the open window suddenly feels chilly. Kameron senses I'm cold and covers us both with a sheet before she takes off the blindfold and removes the cuffs.

It's like I've been reduced to nothing, because I feel so light, but at the same time it's like my mind has expanded. Blinking against the faint candlelight, I find her eyes and smile while she takes me in her arms and holds me tight. The closeness I feel then is overwhelming. It's like I've given her a piece of myself, like I've offered up a part of me I didn't even know I had. Trying not to overanalyze how I feel, I wrap my arms around her in return and let out a deep sigh of contentment, because whatever just happened is bigger than me.

19

"**M**orning, babe."

My eyes flutter open and I smile when I see Kameron looking at me. She's sitting beside me on the bed with a laptop on her lap. "Hey." Stretching myself, I hold back a yawn and turn on my side. "Why didn't you wake me sooner?" By the looks of the bright light flooding into the room, the sun is already high in the sky and when I pick up my phone to check the time, I'm surprised to see that it's past midday already.

"I just took the time to do some work, so I can have the rest of the day off to spend with you." Closing the laptop, she puts it aside and scoots down under the covers with me. "Besides, it looked like you really needed to rest after last night."

"Yeah, I suppose I did," I say, and feel myself blush as flashbacks hit me, stirring my desire. I take her hand and kiss it and note how at ease I feel with her. There's no awkwardness or politeness between us. I can be myself here; I'm not trying, and I don't think she is either. We're both grinning like we're each other's biggest fans, grabbing every opportunity to touch each other, constantly craving the contact.

"Trying new things can be both physically and mentally exhausting." Kameron shoots me a heated look and I know she's getting aroused by the memory too. She looks and smells like she's just had a shower and her wet hair is slicked back, emphasizing her boyish sexiness.

"Maybe." I run my hand over her cheek and her neck, marveling at how soft she feels. "But it's also thrilling and exciting and frankly, it's also been eye-opening to me. Thank you."

Kameron shakes her head. "I should be the one to thank you, Ivy. I'm humbled that you put your trust in me and I don't think you have any idea how much I've enjoyed our time together so far." She pauses. "It's been eye-opening to me too."

Her words make my insides dance and I smile. "So, you're taking more time off? That's really sweet, but you don't have to do that for me."

"Who says I'm doing it for you?" Kameron quirks her lips. "Wanting to be with you is entirely selfish on my behalf." She gestures to a bag on the chair by the dressing table. "Steph dropped off some more clothes for you, in case you wanted to venture out today."

"Oh, great. Please thank her from me. I can't believe I didn't hear anything." I wrap my arms around Kameron, thinking I could easily just stay in bed all day with her. My body is stiff and sore though, so I probably need some light exercise of the vertical kind.

Kameron pulls me closer and kisses me, and when I align myself with her body, I realize how clammy I am.

"I think I need a shower." I wiggle myself out of her grip, then shriek in surprise as she tries to pull me back, jutting out her bottom lip while she gives me a pleading look.

"Come on, just five more minutes."

"No, I'm gross." I laugh. "Why don't you come in the shower with me instead?" Clearly, I'm still insatiable—even after the long night we've spent together—as my body shudders at the thought of touching Kameron in the shower again.

Kameron seems to think it's an excellent idea as she jumps out of bed too and follows me to the bathroom. "So you're not sick of me yet?"

"I don't think I could ever get sick of you." I switch on the shower and pull her in for a long make-out session, basking in a whole new kind of happiness. I feel light and totally carefree, nothing on my mind except for the physical craving of having my mouth between her legs and making her scream. Even with the lip balm I applied over a dozen times yesterday, my lips are still sore from all the kissing and I'm starting to think there might not be much left of them by the time I leave.

"My parents used to take me and my brother to this place, but I hadn't been here in about twenty years until a couple of months ago. I guess I've rediscovered it." Kameron smiles at the young woman behind the counter and gives her a thumbs-up about the food. "That's the owner's daughter, she really looks like her mother."

"It's cute." I look around, appreciating the shaded, flower-filled terrace outside a café that is situated on a quiet corner close to her apartment. Kameron showed me around her neighborhood until we ended up here for lunch, and I can tell she's proud of where she lives. She took my hand as we walked, and I'm not sure why walking hand in hand in broad daylight felt so strange. Perhaps because that's something only couples do at this time of day, or perhaps because I feel myself growing closer to her with every minute we spend together, and I'm worried I'll get sucked in too deep. Now she's sitting opposite me, and even though our knees are touching, the small distance between us seems too much. "Why haven't you been back?" As I say it, I silently curse myself and hold up a hand. "Sorry, that was a silly question."

"No, it's not a silly question; because it's not necessarily painful being here." Kameron takes a moment, carefully considering her words. "Have you ever been back to a place after years and years, and you get this funny feeling? Like when you pass your old high school, or a place you used to spend a lot of time, or an old friend's house—one that you don't see anymore—and it doesn't feel right to be there because everything is different and it belongs to another time in your life?"

"I know what you mean." I think of my grandmother's old house, which I always avoid walking past on my way to my parent's house. The new owners have taken down the beautiful big tree in the front yard and it makes me feel sad. "If I revisit places that belong in my past—even the ones with good memories—it reminds me of the fact that everything changes, that nothing lasts forever."

"Exactly. It wasn't the same coming here without my family, so I avoided it. It just gave me that strange sense of déjà vu, and I still get it with a lot of places, like the local library and the ice cream stand by the river."

"So why now?"

Kameron grins as she points to her empty plate. "The food. It's really, really good."

I laugh too and stab my fork through the last piece of waffle. "Yeah, it is."

"Right?" She sits back and pushes her plate to the side. "The owner's daughter took over and she renovated it a couple of months ago. I walked past and I was curious to see what she'd done to the place, so I sat down for lunch and the buttermilk pancakes tasted just as good as they did when I was twelve. Apart from the amazing pancakes, everything is totally different now, so I don't get sucked back into old memories."

"Do you miss them? Your parents and your brother?"

"Every day. But I'm not sad anymore, if that's what you mean."

"What were they like?" I know I might be overstepping with my probing questions, but I find myself wanting to know everything there is to know about her.

"My parents were nice. Decent people. Maybe not the most caring parents in the traditional sense, but I know they loved me. My brother and I always got ourselves into trouble, I don't know how they put up with us." Kameron chuckles but her smile doesn't reach her eyes. "They had big plans for me—my mother always dreamed of me being a doctor, but I never went to university. I could have; they left me money, and quite a fair amount, too, but I joined the army instead because I wanted to get away after their death and it was the right decision at the time."

"I'm sure that most of all, they just wanted you to be happy," I say. "They would certainly be proud of you now. You seem like a good person."

"I hope so." Kameron shakes her head, deciding she's done talking about serious matters. "Well, if it's not too warm for you, how about I get the check so we can finish the tour?"

20

———

"What else is in that bag?" I ask, poking it with my toe as my leg is dangling over the edge of the bed in an attempt to cool down. It's a sultry night, the warmth of the evening enveloping us like a soft cloud. We could switch on the air-conditioning, but we both prefer to have the windows open and let the breeze flow through the room. Anyway, the heat suits my mood and it feels fitting to be hot and sweaty.

"You mean, what else *was* in that bag?" Cameron turns on her side and arches a brow while she trails a hand up and down my naked body. "You're about to find out."

Her words make me gulp because I have no idea what she's hinting at. "Okay. Show me."

We've had a wonderful afternoon but knowing we didn't have that much time left together, we ventured home before dinner and ended up having a very, very long and unforgettable shower together. Being dressed almost seems like a waste of time in her company, and I'm pretty sure Kameron feels the same way. I don't even think I care if I'm just her flavor of the week, or her new favorite toy, as I can't say I mind being subjected to multiple orgasms a day.

Kameron points to the nightstand, where five red candles are burning in silver candlesticks. "They were in the bag." They're the only source of light in here, apart from the moon and the city lights outside, and the atmosphere in the room is dreamy and romantic, with the white curtains blowing in and the soft music in the background.

"Candles..." I frown, not understanding what she's getting at.

"Yes. They're special candles."

"Oh." My eyes shift from the candles to Cameron and back and as she gets up on her knees and straddles me, her flickering shadow growing on the wall like that of a ghost. This feels dangerous but I'm distracted by her wetness against my belly and her full breasts hanging over me.

"We've established your erogenous zones like the cold..." she wets her lips. "Now let's see how they feel about heat." A smile plays around her lips as she picks up one of the candles, then carefully drips some of the wax onto her wrist. "This particular wax won't burn your skin." She looks at me and holds it up, dripping more onto her hand to show it's not hurting her. Although she doesn't make a sound, I do see her flinch a little. "Want to try?"

I swallow hard as I watch it set on her skin, leaving a small red mark after she peels it off. I can't say this has been on my bucket list, but I'm curious and willing to give anything a try because so far, she's surprised me over and over, intuitively knowing what I want before I know it myself. "Okay. But be careful."

"I'm always careful." Her voice is soothing, almost comforting, telling me I'm safe with her. The light of the candle is reflected in her eyes when she holds it up in front of her. "I won't tie you up for this; I don't want you to panic. Just stay still on your back and keep your hands above your head."

I nod and feel a tremble run through me as I place my hands on the pillow above me. The idea of pushing boundaries both scares me and fascinates me; I've never been the adventurous type but with Kameron, I know I'm in good hands. Still, the rush of fear that hits me as she lifts the candle is hard to ignore.

Slowly, she tilts it over my left breast, her lips parting as the first droplet of wax hits my skin.

I hold my breath, then gasp at the sharp sting and exhale deeply as I watch the red blood-like blob dribble into an oval shape, then set above my nipple. It hurts, but the pain shoots right to my pussy, and sends a delicious twitch to my clit.

Kameron shifts back, giving me just what I need by moving her weight to where it has most impact. Having her wetness on my shaven pussy is driving me insane and it's almost impossible to keep my hands to myself. I want to rub the sore skin on my breast as well as touch her, and it's making me restless.

"No. Keep them where they are," she says when she notices the subtle shift in my hands. "Are you okay?"

"Yeah." I'm not sure why I say this with a hint of humor in my voice. Maybe because I never expected this to turn me on, or maybe because this is so not me that it's funny.

Kameron smiles as she tilts the candle again, dripping more wax onto my breast. Her immense arousal is obvious in her expression. She watches me gasp and moan, and bends over me to grab my wrists. When the wax hits my nipple, I cry out, and she shifts to my other breast, repeating the ritual.

I'm a heaving conflicted mess; my mind telling me that I shouldn't be enjoying this, and my body in a state of ecstasy, screaming out for release.

"Lower," I beg.

Kameron lets go of my wrists and I curse when the wax hits my surprisingly sensitive belly. "You asked for it," she says with a grin as she gets on her knees in between my legs. "Want me to stop?" Holding the candle away from me, she spreads my legs apart and without warning, runs her tongue through my folds.

"Fuck!!!" I jerk my hips up to meet her mouth, but she pulls away. I arch my back, heaving and moaning, and it's then that she lifts the candle again, enticing me to choose between pleasure and pain.

"Want this?"

Knowing what's coming, I close my eyes tight and hold my breath. "Do it." By this point I don't really care if it hurts; because I know it will also feel really, really good, and I need her to release me of the pent-up sexual energy that's threatening to send me into hysteria.

When the hot wax falls onto my swollen pussy lips, I cry out and throw my head back. My hand shoots down, but she catches it and places it back over my head. It's painful, but at the same time I'm close to climaxing and I have no idea if I want her to stop, or to continue.

Taking the decision for me, she carefully places the candle back in the candlestick, then kisses me hard. Her fingers caress my face and her thigh moves between my legs, putting pressure against my aching pussy. I'm not sure if I can take any more teasing when she raises herself and studies me, clearly happy with her work. The red wax has set on my chest in dripping streaks. If someone were to walk in now, they would surely think something horrible had happened to me, but nothing could be further from the truth.

"Please let me come," I beg as I look up at her.

Kameron doesn't answer as she roams her hands over my body, my nipples stiffening painfully under the hard pools of crimson wax. Her hands seem to be enjoying the sensation as she taps her nails repeatedly over my breasts—each vibration ratcheting up the level of pleasure. I suck a breath in through my teeth as she begins to slowly peel off the wax—each slow stinging tug on my skin igniting my clit in the process. When she moves lower toward my belly, removing one of the last pieces, she hesitates. "Just one bit left." Reaching between my legs, she fondles me while she rips it off, her lips parting at the pool of wetness she finds. "I think you're ready."

"Ready for what?" I'm starting to worry now, because this can't possibly be just foreplay, and my breath hitches when she reaches into the bag and takes out the strap-on.

I watch her put it on and want to clench my thighs together at the sight, but she's lying between them, preventing me from doing that. I'm so wet that I can feel the dampness against my inner thigh as the breeze blows in.

"Is this okay with you?" she asks, looking down at me.

"Yes." I couldn't possibly want it more, but I'm also curiously nervous, and even though I know it's silly, I can't help but feel like I'm about to lose my virginity all over again.

"Hmm..." She lowers herself on top of me and kisses me softly. "I love that I'm going to be your first." Reaching between us, Kameron guides the shaft up and down over my throbbing pussy and smiles when I throw my head back and moan. It's slippery against my lips, coated in my juices. Slowly, she pushes inside me, and I hold onto her tight, moaning louder as I feel it stretching me open. The warm sense of fullness causes an intense rush and makes my blood pump vigorously, awakening my nerves to a higher state.

"Look at me," she says, and takes both my hands, lacing our fingers together above my head.

Fighting to keep my eyes open, I focus on her handsome face. She's biting her bottom lip and a frown appears between her brows as she thrusts into me and moans. I love knowing that this feels good for her too, and I move my hips along with hers until we're so in sync that it's like we're floating together, seeking pleasure and beyond, without limitations.

Our bodies fit perfectly, and her full breasts against my chest and her hands grasping mine fills me with a glow warmer than the sun. She's everything that matters right now.

The fullness and friction against my clit increase as Kameron thrusts deeper and deeper, like she's wanting to become a part of me. She is. We're one, and her bed starts creaking as we move faster until we cry out, releasing our joint tension. My hands clasp hers so hard they become numb, and my walls are grasping onto the shaft, sucking it in while my eyes never leave hers.

We're shaking, panting, moaning, still moving, even after our orgasm has subsided, basking in the aftershocks and the quiet closeness that confirms how good we are together.

21

———

"**A**re you thirsty?"

I nod and swallow hard, noting my throat is dry. "Yeah."

Kameron kisses my forehead before she gets up. "Water? Lemonade? Tea? Wine?"

"Water would be great," I say, finally feeling a little bit of energy rush back through my body. I was limp for a while, thinking I'd never be able to move again, but when she leaves the room, I feel an urge to follow her. Intimacy comes in all kinds of forms, and what we've just done, including the cuddling after, is intimate beyond belief to me, and I miss her already.

Wrapping myself in her bedsheets, I find my feet and tiptoe into the kitchen, then silently watch her from the door. She adds ice to a glass, then shakes her head and swaps the glass out for a bigger one before pouring the water in. I have no idea why this affects me, but I feel real tenderness when I look at her doing mundane things.

Sensing my presence, she turns and smiles at me. "Hey. Are you okay?"

"Yeah. Just watching you." It's a simple statement but I can tell by her expression that she knows it means a whole lot more than that. She's wearing a blue toweling robe, her hair is a hot mess and I notice her hand is trembling a little as she hands me the glass.

"Just watching, huh?"

At that very moment, I know I'm in trouble. Taking a long drink, I try to hide the fact that I'm crazy about her. That I'm crushing on her madly and deeply. That I don't want to say goodbye, and that I don't want this to end, despite what I've been telling myself. I'm just not ready yet.

"It's a shame you have to leave on Thursday," she says as if reading my mind, pouring herself a glass of water, too.

I lean against the counter, never taking my eyes off her. There's a hint of discomfort in her demeanor, but something tells me that's a good thing. She's not used to women hanging around, but she wants me to stay and she has no idea how to deal with that.

Kameron walks over to me and puts her glass down before she lifts me onto the counter and steps between my legs. "Hmm..." Her eyes shift from me to the ceiling and back before her expression softens. "I think I adore you," she says, and her words linger between us like she's just fired a bullet and I'm waiting for it to hit.

It comes so unexpected that I don't know what to say. Her words fill me with warmth but the little voice in the back of my mind reminds me that it's not the first time a woman has said that to me. My ex was particularly smooth like that, and it was only a matter of time before she betrayed me.

During the long silence that follows, I pull her closer and search for ways to express myself. I can't seem to fully function when she's near though, and her dark eyes make me lose my train of thought entirely. "I adore you too. But..."

"But?"

"But I don't know you." I pause. "And... I have serious trust issues, so whatever this is, I need to take it very, very slow. Sex is one thing but exchanging words like that, it scares me."

"It wasn't my intention to scare you, it just came out." Kameron brushes a lock of hair away from my face. "But I meant what I said, so please don't take it lightly, coming from me." Her hand curls around my neck and her fingers grazing the fine hairs there send shivers down my spine. "Why do you have trust issues? I'm sorry, you don't have to talk about it if you don't want to," she quickly adds.

"No... it's fine." I've done everything to push the bad experiences I've had to the back of my mind; I haven't even told my family why Emily and I suddenly split up, and Tessa is the only one who knows. But maybe it's time that I face the music and tell someone else. "Emily, my ex, moved in with me." Noting that saying her name doesn't hurt anymore, I feel encouraged to continue. "One day, a strange woman showed up on our doorstep. I was supposed to be at a gig, but I had a bad cold, so I'd cancelled. Emily opened the door and as soon as I heard her whisper, I knew something was wrong. It was just this uncomfortable feeling, you know, so I got out of bed and walked into the hallway, where I saw her talking to a woman. She was pretty; tall, blonde, curvy—everything that I'm not—and she was begging Emily to leave me, to run away with her, as she put it. Even when she saw me, she didn't give up. She was right in front of me, talking to my girlfriend like I wasn't even there. Little did I know they'd already been seeing each other for seven months behind my back." I shrug and meet Kameron's eyes.

"Emily didn't need to make any decisions of course; I did that for her."

"I'm so sorry that happened to you. Emily was clearly insane."

"Maybe. But there's a pattern here. Before Emily, there was Milda, and Milda had someone on the side, too. At least she had the decency to confess, but not until I confronted her with her odd behavior. Tessa always claimed there was something off about her, because she attended more dance classes and courses at night than kids of pushy helicopter parents, but I didn't want to hear about it. Anyway, turns out she was right." I shrug. It's strange how easy it is to talk about it now. I don't know if it's because I'm in the middle of this steamy affair that makes everything in my past seem insignificant, or because time really does heal.

"That must have burned you bad," Kameron says.

"It did. For years, I wondered what was wrong with me, why I wasn't good enough for either of them. I just threw myself into the relationships, hopeful and in love, and I never doubted that I was safe. We didn't argue much, in fact, I was happy with both Milda and Emily, and I thought they were happy with me too. It took me a while to realize it was on them and not me, but I still have serious trust issues when it comes to women and people in general."

"Well, I hope you know there's nothing wrong with you." Kameron leans in to kiss me softly. "I think you're amazing."

"Thank you. I think you're amazing, too." My eyes fall onto a photograph on the fridge, one of Kameron and her brother, and I suddenly feel ashamed of myself for pouring my heart out. "I'm sorry," I say, shaking my head. "My stupid problems must seem terribly shallow to you, after what you've been through."

A kind smile settles over her face as she shakes her head

while leaning in and wrapping her arms around me. "Everyone has problems, and everyone's problems are valid. We'll always be a product of our past, no matter how hard we try not to let it rule our lives, and I totally understand how those two women ruined your trust for the rest of us. And my past has had a major influence on who I am today, too, I'm not going to deny that. I've lost everyone that was truly close to me and so I'm very careful letting people in too... I've certainly never gone looking for anyone special." She squeezes me tightly and sighs. "But sometimes things just happen to us for a reason."

"Yeah." I melt into her embrace and close my eyes.

"So, what are we going to do?"

"I don't know." I slowly pull out of the hug and I think it over as we exchange a slightly awkward glance. She's clearly not used to this closeness and I'm not going to jump all in either. "Do we have to decide now?"

"No..."

"Then why don't we see how we feel tomorrow and take it from there?"

"One day at a time?" Kameron nods. "I can do that. I just wish I had more time with you."

22

"Are you serious?" Tessa's eyes are wide with surprise as I report back to her after spending two days and three glorious nights with Kameron. She had work commitments today, and I'm finally seeing Tessa alone after we've come up for air following days spent getting lost in ourselves with our new lovers.

We've met up at a coffee place close to her apartment, famous for its beignets. They're delicious but hard to eat without getting powdered sugar everywhere and I'm glad I got changed into a white T-shirt and jeans at her place before we came here. It's strange to sit here with Tessa—it reminds me that real life is waiting for me, because Tessa is a part of my real life.

"Mmmhmm," I mumble as I lick my fingers. I'm not sure why I've told Tessa everything, but I've discovered so many new things about myself that I needed to talk about it. Besides, there's no shame with Tessa. She's seen me at my best and at my worst and she knows me through and through.

Kameron and I have been up during the nights having

sex and then sleeping for most of the days and even though I make a living as a nightclub singer, I don't lead this kind of life in New York. I'm usually in bed by one or two am, but only on nights that I'm working, and I get up around ten and clean the house and do chores like everyone else. On weekends I often have lunch at my parents' house, and my brother keep me busy when they need a babysitter for their twins.

These past days have been surreal in so many ways and talking about it might help me understand my instant attraction and crush on a woman I've only just met. So far, I haven't come to any new insights though, and the only explanation I can think of is that there really is such a thing as instant chemistry.

"I didn't take you for a tie-me-up-and-spank-me-girl." Tessa giggles. "But hey, that woman is hot. She had this commanding air about her at the party; I can see why you're attracted to her."

"I'm so into her," I admit. "But it's not about the tying up and the spanking." I wince as I say it out loud because it sounds alien coming from my mouth. "We just have this energy together. It's highly sexual; I've never had that before with anyone. Just being in the same room with her turns me on."

"Totally get that." Tessa smirks. "Steph and I have had a lot of fun in the bedroom, too. She's very talented, and apparently, so am I." She bats her lashes and thrusts out her chest.

"I know you are," I say, ruffling her feathers, just to make her happy. Tessa and I weren't a good match sexually, at least not in my opinion, but she doesn't need to know I felt that way. "Where is Stephanie?"

"Gone to work. She's a party organizer." Tessa takes a

bite of her beignet, covering her nose in a cloud of powdered sugar. Chewing slowly, her eyes widen. "Damn, this is good. I was only going to have one small piece." She sighs in frustration. "See? This is why I don't order sweet stuff. Because I love it and then I eat it all."

I laugh and shake my head. "But that's what it's for. It's not going to kill you." Sitting back, I enjoy the sun on my face. "Live a little. Wasn't that what you said you wanted to do when you moved here?"

"You're right. I might as well indulge before I go back to work next week." Tessa takes another bite, then continues with a mouthful. "Anyway, pretty cool, right? That I'm dating a party organizer."

I'm not sure if Stephanie would consider what they're doing as 'dating', but I'm not going to rain on her parade by mentioning that. "So, what kind of parties does she organize?" I let out a loud snicker. "The naked kind?"

"That too." Tessa leans in and lowers her voice. "I'm not sure if I'm supposed to tell you this, but she kind of let it slip that she works for Countess Montgomery."

"Really? She said that?"

Tessa purses her lips and hesitates. "Well, she didn't let it slip as much. I was sitting on her couch while she was having a shower and there was a pile of paperwork on the coffee table..."

"Oh God, don't tell me you went through her stuff."

"I didn't go through it; I just moved the top letter aside so I could read the one underneath. It was a rental agreement between Countess C. Montgomery and some other person." Tessa shrugs. "I swapped them around and when she came back, I casually asked her about it."

I frown, remembering my conversations with Kameron. "So, she knows the Countess?"

"I'm not sure, she was very vague about it, so I stopped enquiring as I shouldn't have snooped in the first place."

"No, you shouldn't have," I say. "But it's interesting."

"Hmm..." Tessa's face drops then. "Why would she be so secretive about it? Do you think something could be going on between them?"

"I wouldn't worry about it," I say, trying to put her at ease. "I'm sure there's a reason she doesn't want to share, and according to Kameron, Countess Montgomery is the best kept secret of New Orleans, so she's probably just protecting her client's identity.

"Hmm... yes, that makes sense." Tessa takes a napkin from the holder between us and wipes her nose. "Anyway, now that we have some time to ourselves, what do you want to do today?"

"I don't know," I say, and take a sip of my coffee. Tessa and I were supposed to explore the city together, but I'm tired and my muscles ache. I can feel where Kameron's been and although it's the best kind of ache, I'm not sure if I can handle walking for hours. "Honestly, I think I just want to chill out. Maybe go for a short walk and enjoy the sunshine in a park or something."

Tessa lets out a sigh of relief. "Thank God, I'm so glad you said that. I haven't slept much either. Isn't it nice to be in love again, though?"

"Tessa, we're not in love." I manage to suppress an eye roll. Tessa is always getting carried away and I suspect she's already picking out her wedding dress. "We only met these women on Saturday. It's just an infatuation."

"Are you saying you don't care if you never see her again?"

"I'm saying that I'm under no illusion that this is going anywhere. With me and Kameron, I mean. You live here, and you and Tessa can see each other anytime you want. It's different with us and besides, I don't think Kameron is the relationship type. She told me she really likes me and I won't deny that I feel close to her, but her phone is constantly ringing and although she never picks up, I can see the names that light up are almost always women's."

"But now she's met you. Maybe you've changed things for her."

I shake my head. "Trust me, she's just getting sucked into this, like me. And I'm having such a good time that I'm totally fine with that. After being heartbroken and single for a year, I really needed this, but I doubt it will turn into something serious."

"You could be wrong," Tessa, the eternal optimist says.

Remembering our moment in the kitchen, a little sparkle of hope makes me smile. "I could be. We'll see how it works out, but the reality is, I'm flying back to New York tomorrow."

Tessa juts out her bottom lip. "But you'll come and visit me again, right? So it's not like you won't come back here." She's not giving up. I know she has visions of me moving to New Orleans, and of the four of us living happily ever after, going on holiday together and attending each other's weddings, looking after each other's children and God knows what else.

"Of course I'll visit again." Sometimes, I wish I was a hopeless romantic like Tessa, but life has thrown me curve-balls that have made me downbeat in the love department. "But let's not get carried away, shall we?"

23

_____

I'm waiting on a corner of the French Quarter in town, where Kameron asked me to meet her after work. Fussing over my hair in the reflection of a storefront, I note that although we saw each other this morning, I'm feeling nervous about seeing her again. It's all so new and exciting, and my heart is racing as I scan the passers-by for a sign of her.

I've changed into a black dress and heels, and I'm wearing new lingerie that I bought with Tessa today. She convinced me to splash out and now I'm glad I did, because the strappy black balconette bra and matching Brazilian panties fit me like a glove and look great with the hold-ups and garter belt by the same French brand.

Even though no one can see the filmy fabric, I know I'm wearing it and that's enough to make me feel very sensual. I have a feeling Kameron is going to like the surprise, too, and I can hardly wait for her to undress me.

My face lights up when I spot her waving as she rushes toward me.

"Sorry I'm late. It's been a little hectic, but everything's taken care of now and I've put Daisy in charge of the job tonight, so I'm all yours." Kameron gives me an approving glance-over. "You look ravishing."

"Thank you. You look great, too." I shoot her a flirty smile before she leans in and kisses me. I see she's changed, too, and I feel special that she's done that for me. The black pantsuit she left in this morning has been replaced by jeans, a casual checked shirt and a navy blazer that make her look incredibly attractive.

Running my hands through her hair, I deepen the kiss because I simply can't resist. Her mouth feels just perfect on mine, and the soft moan that escapes her sends butterflies to my core.

"I've missed you," she murmurs against my mouth. "And since you're leaving tomorrow, I thought I should at least take you out on a date. You know... just you and me. No Steph to embarrass me all night."

I laugh and take her hand as we walk into an alleyway. "A date, huh?"

"Yes. Is that too serious for you? We can just call it dinner, if you prefer."

"No, not at all. Where are you taking me?" I frown as she suddenly stops and greets a woman standing on top of a set of steep stairs, descending from what looks like a hole in the wall. There's no sign or menu outside, only the hostess who checks Kameron's name against the reservations.

"Miss Kameron, it's nice to have you back," she says, then gestures to the stairs.

"This is my favorite restaurant and after tonight, I have no doubt it will be yours too." Kameron seems to know a lot of people, as she greets other patrons and makes small talk with the members of staff we pass on the way to our table in the back.

"You seem pretty confident about the food," I say, but I can already see I'm going to love this place. It's packed and noisy, the sound of raised, happy voices ringing through the air. The dishes that are being carried through the restaurant smell and look delicious and the staff seems very personable.

"I am. It's one of the oldest family owned restaurants in New Orleans. It's been passed on for four generations and so have the recipes." She pulls out a chair for me and takes the seat opposite. "I gathered since you're from New York, you might want to try some southern soul food."

"You guessed right. I asked Tessa to take me somewhere for southern food when I arrived, but we ended up in a sushi bar." I roll my eyes and laugh. "Tessa has been dieting for as long as I can remember; it's kind of annoying to go to a restaurant with her. Anyway, you witnessed that firsthand last night."

"Yes, Steph is like that too, so at least they've got one thing in common," Kameron jokes. "I hope *you're* not on a diet though; this food is going to be rich."

"Bring it on; I don't do diets." My mouth is already watering as I glance over the menu our waitress hands us.

"Good." Kameron orders a bottle of wine, then looks me over and licks her lips suggestively. "Because your body is delicious, and I wouldn't want to have less of it, especially in that tight dress you're wearing."

I meet her heated gaze and feel arousal stirring. I know she likes my body; she's made that more than clear since the night we met. The gym is not my favorite place in the world, but I've always been happy in my own skin. "Oh yeah? You like my dress?"

"I like it very much." Kameron's gaze lowers to my

cleavage and remembering her mouth on my breasts makes me shiver.

"I think you're going to like what's underneath it even more." I was worried I'd be overdressed at first, but people here seem to be wearing whatever they feel like. When I spot a man in a skirt and a woman in an electric pink coverall, I decide it doesn't matter.

"Mmm..." Kameron sinks down in her chair and pushes her foot between mine under the table. "I can't wait to unwrap you. Will you still have enough energy left for me tonight?"

"Of course." I meet her eyes and try not to show how much her comment affects me but fail miserably. My smile says it all; I've been fantasizing about her all day. Not seeing her while she was at work made me realize how much I'm going to miss her and it's making me feel things I shouldn't be feeling at this point. "What about you? Do you still have what it takes?"

"For you, always."

"You charmer." I look down at her phone when it lights up. I don't mean to look but it's hard not to, what with all the different names that constantly appear. *Mandy Loveless*. "Seems like Mandy has a lot of energy for you too," I joke, although I can't deny that by now, it's starting to sting a little.

Kameron puts her phone in her pocket. "Sorry, bad habit of keeping it on the table. I don't really go on dates normally, so I just forget about my manners." She shrugs. "I'm really sorry, it's disrespectful to you but I swear I haven't been in contact with any other women since the Black and White masquerade, even though it might not look that way."

"It's fine," I say. "You don't owe me anything."

"I'm not sure I agree with that. If nothing else, I owe you

my undivided attention." Kameron tilts her head and adds: "I respect all women and don't play games with them. I make a point of being very clear with them from the beginning and they know not to expect anything more than the occasional night from me. But I like you. And I mean, I really, really like you." She shrugs. "But you already know that."

"Yeah..."

"Have you thought about our talk last night?" She asks when I remain quiet.

"Yes." Again, I fall silent. It's not that I don't know what I want; I want her and only her. It's not just my body screaming out for her anymore; my mind has been consumed with Kameron. But saying that will make me vulnerable and that's not a place I like to be, given my history with women. The way she looks at me puts me at ease though, and so I finally find the courage to answer honestly. "All day," I admit. "In fact, I haven't stopped thinking about you all day."

"Same." Kameron's gaze is focused on me as a serious frown appears between her brows. "I really think we should explore where this could lead. It would be a shame not to."

There's a long silence between us as I process what's happening here because despite her sweet words, I was convinced the fact that I live in New York was one of the reasons why she liked me. Nice and simple. Temporary. No strings. "What exactly are you saying?"

"Well, I'm not quite sure how this would work, but we could maybe call each other and visit each other and see how that goes?" Kameron holds up a hand. "If you don't want that, I totally understand and I promise you, I'll leave you alone. But if you do..." Her voice trails off and for the first time, her voice has a tremble to it. "Then I want you to know that I'm all in." She pats her pocket, holding her phone. "I swear, I'll throw my phone in the Mississippi River."

I laugh, grateful for the joke that takes some of the pressure off the conversation. "That seems a little extreme, but I appreciate the thought," I say, leaning in closer. "So, you would call this a relationship of some sorts?"

"Yes, I would call it exactly that. A relationship. And, well... I'd like you to..." Kameron shakes her head and rolls her eyes as if she can't compute what is coming out of her mouth. "I'd like you to be my girlfriend." She shoots me a crooked smile and I almost melt at how clumsy the words roll off her tongue.

"Have you ever been in a relationship?" I ask.

"No."

"You're forty-seven and you've never been in a relationship..." I pause. "Why now? Why me?"

"Because you're different. I feel different with you and I'm crazy about you." Kameron holds up her hands. "There. I've said it. I'm crazy about you and I'd like to date you. Think about it, I don't need an answer now. Just don't forget about me."

"I won't. You know I won't." I'm so focused on her that I almost jump up when the waitress appears at my side.

"Drinks, ladies?"

"Sure." Kameron clears her throat and orders a bottle of red wine. She's blushing and it's super cute.

"Will you order the food?" I ask her. "I have no idea what half of this is, but I'm sure everything is amazing." Sitting back, I brace myself for an interesting dinner. Here was I, suspecting I was nothing more than a name in her phone to her, but nothing could have been further from the truth. I tell myself not to overthink this. Kameron makes me feel alive, happy, and desired, and if that's not enough to give her a chance, I don't know what is.

24

We're walking along the path that runs beside the river and it's a beautiful sight, with the city lights scattered along the bend in the river. The quiet sound of the water splashing against the rocks, the midnight blue starry sky and Kameron's hand in mine makes for a night to remember, and I smile, my belly fluttering after our talk. I feel like I'm on top of the world, like I'm charged by the electricity that sparks between us.

"I love it here," I say, watching a steamboat pass, guided by the roving spotlights on the embankment. "It's such a fun city, yet at the same time, it's so peaceful."

"Yes, there's definitely something for everyone. I missed it while I was in the army, and whenever I'm away, it's always good to come back."

Our romantic moment is interrupted when Kameron's phone vibrates again, and she lets out a sigh.

"I think you should pick up and at least explain to Mandy Loveless that you're busy." I say it with a smirk because it sounds like a stripper name and I wouldn't be surprised if she actually was a stripper. Also, I'm dying to hear what Kameron has to say to her. I wonder if she'll tell her the truth or make up an excuse. I imagine her picking up and walking away from me to take the call in private. Perhaps she'll say that she's working, but that she's available next week, or even on Thursday, after I've left. Immediately, I feel ashamed of thinking the worst of her yet again. So far, she's only proven to be kind, thoughtful, fun and considerate, and I curse myself for still not being able to let her in, to trust her. Maybe it's time. Maybe I should just join her for the ride and see where this goes. If it works out, it will have been the best decision of my life. If we crash and burn and I find out that she ended up in the arms of Mandy Loveless after all, well, then I've had an amazing few days with an amazing woman. I might be a little crushed, but not much harm will be done as I'm sure I'll find out soon enough what she's made of.

"It's okay. Mandy's like me, she'll have another dozen women or so that she can call. But I'm sorry."

"Hey, as I said, I'm not here to judge you." I take in a deep breath and raise my gaze to look at her. "And what we discussed over dinner, well…" Squeezing her hand, I stop and pull her closer. "I'd like to date you too. I want to try."

"Really?" Kameron's smile widens and seeing her so happy makes my insides dance with joy. "I'm…" Her phone vibrates again, and this time, she does take it out of her pocket. "Damn it," she mutters.

"Answer," I say.

Kameron shakes her head and looks skyward before she holds it up, then throws it in the river with force. It bounces off the surface, splashes hard, and I vaguely see the light blink a couple of times before it sinks into the river's dark depths.

I slam my hand in front of my mouth and gasp. "Did you

really just throw away your phone?" It seems terribly impulsive, but she doesn't look like she regrets it.

"Hey, I needed you to see how much I like you." Kameron grins. "It's just my personal phone. I have a separate work phone, and if distant relatives need to reach me, they'll know where to find me."

"Okay..." I laugh and wrap my arms around her. "You must really like me."

"As a matter of fact, I do." Kameron cups my face and kisses me sweetly. It's tender and so soft that I can barely feel it, but its effect is mesmerizing and causes more emotions than I can handle. Arousal, attraction, affection, excitement, closeness, fear...

I run my hands over her face in return and kiss her back. From her reaction, I know she's shocked, too. It's like something has changed between us, like the exchange of a few simple words have elevated the chemistry between us to a whole new level. I need the warmth of her body, tight against mine, and I want to hold her and make out with her forever.

Our kiss is slow and sensual, and I'm savoring the moment that I'll undoubtedly remember forever, no matter what happens. Our dark silhouettes against the river and the nights' sky, the moon; full and bright above us. Her hands on my skin, her lips on mine, the way she inhales deep as if drinking me in. It causes a storm to brew inside me, but I hold back, cherishing the tenderness between us.

I know she feels it too, and it frightens me more than the games we played last night, because I know I'm letting her in. I've opened up the gates to my heart, just a little, and she's swimming inside me, exploring my most vulnerable place and building a bridge of connection.

Unable to let her cross that bridge, I pull away and shake my head incredulously as I stare up at her. "What was that?"

"I'm not sure." Kameron looks confused too. "It was..." The horn of the steamboat cuts through the silence, and it brings us back to the present. She takes my hand. "Come on, let's go home."

25

"This is new to me." Kameron places a cup of tea in front of me and sits down next to me on her couch. "This..." She waves a finger between us.

I sense that she's never had deep feelings for a woman before, at least not anything more than the superficial kind, but this isn't the first time for me. The intensity of our connection though, is new to me too, and I'm baffled by how close we've grown in only a matter of days. "Are you okay with that?"

"Yeah." She takes a careful sip of her tea. "It feels amazing, but I'm also terrified."

"That's normal. You don't want to get hurt; trust me, I've been there." She's opening up to me and I feel privileged to witness it. "But honestly, I've never felt this before either—this level of intensity—and I'm terrified too.

I feel sad and although I'm trying not to, I'm counting down our last hours in my head. *Fourteen to go.* I'm thinking how lucky I've been to have met her, purely by chance. If Tessa hadn't found that invitation on the floor, we wouldn't have gone to the party. If Kameron hadn't decided she wanted to have some fun with a stranger, and hadn't slipped that key into her pocket, I wouldn't be here right now, and I would never have felt the way I do now. Hell, if Tessa hadn't been offered a job in New Orleans, I might not have visited this wonderful city. And if I were still with Emily... well, I'm just glad I'm not because now that I know how good it can be with someone else, it's hard to understand how I was involved with a woman who was so cold and passionless for three years. Compared to Kameron, all women seem insignificant now, and if this doesn't work out, I suspect there's little hope for me in the dating department because no one will be able to live up to her. No one could ever be as perfect for me as she is. All the choices we've made have led us here, to this moment, and I realize how precious it is.

I don't want to play games right now and I sense Kameron doesn't want that either. She's lit candles in the living room and put music on and it's nice here, in front of the river-facing window. Tonight, I don't want to be restrained. I want to be able to touch her, to indulge in the softness of her skin. The steamy discussions we've had over dessert have faded to the background, overtaken by the sadness of our looming goodbye.

"Come here." Kameron pats her lap and I shift on the couch to straddle her. Her hair feels wonderful and I keep messing it up because I simply can't resist running my hands through it whenever I get a chance. "I want to feel you," she says as if reading my mind. When she pulls my dress off over my head, I'm left in my new lingerie, and her eyes sparkle at the sight. "Well, damn, I didn't see this coming." Wedging a finger under the elastic of my garter belt, she pulls at it until it snaps back.

"I thought you might appreciate it." I blink with feigned innocence and start unbuttoning her shirt, because I want to feel her too. She's gorgeous, looking up at me through hazy eyes, laced with both lust and tenderness. Leaning in, I run my tongue over her bottom lip and the soft moan that escapes her fills me with heat.

She pulls me close and kisses me deeper while she runs her hands over my back and unclasps my bra. When it falls off, she takes me in, tracing the subtle curves of my breasts as if seeing them for the first time. The way she looks at me is different from last night, like she wants to savor me—the same way as I want to savor her.

I lean back in her strong grip, allowing her to kiss them and fold her lips around my nipples. The warmth of her mouth feels amazing as her fingers skim my waistline. Something has shifted in our energy since our walk home, and as we fall into a passionate embrace, there's a whole new sense of pureness and innocence to what we're doing. There's no power game this time, and no relentless teasing. We're just giving and taking, taking and giving until I don't know where I end and she begins. She's pressing all of her into all of me, as if holding me isn't enough, and I allow myself to sink into her embrace. Her arms are like a cocoon and being held has never felt this good.

"Let me undress you too," I whisper, and take off her shirt and her bra, then push her down into the pillows. Kissing my way down her body, I take off her jeans and her boxers, memorizing every inch of her skin, feeling tipsy from her scent. I want to hold onto this until I next see her, capture this moment so I can close my eyes and recall how it feels, how her voice sounds, how her body reacts to my caress.

Kameron moans and writhes underneath me but stops me when I'm about to descend between her legs. "Let's go to bed. This couch is too small, and I need space to make love to you."

Our hands are everywhere, our kisses deep and passionate, causing soft murmurs and moans to ring through the bedroom. We're lying on our sides, facing each other, our legs entangled, and even our feet are rubbing as we explore each other all over again.

Kameron strokes the inside of my thigh and brings her hand between my legs, softly skimming her fingers over my sensitive skin. The featherlight touch is driving me wild and I buck my hips to meet them as they curl around the edge of my panties.

Lowering my hand between us, I find her wet and ready, and she gasps when I caress her clit, barely touching her. Going on her reaction, I know it won't take much, the way her short breaths are becoming heavy and her dark eyes are narrowing in flaming bliss. Just as I increase pressure and start stroking her, she enters me with two fingers, and it feels so good that I almost forget what I'm doing.

"I want to be inside you too," I murmur against her mouth, and when she doesn't protest, I lower my fingers and inch inside her, just a little.

"Jesus..." Kameron lets out a throaty groan of pleasure and I can tell by her reaction that it's been a very long time since someone did this to her. Her tightness and wet heat drive me wild and as I push deeper, I close my eyes and bask in the sensation of her walls clenching around my fingers.

Nothing could be more beautiful than this moment, as we start thrusting into each other in a lazy pace, our lips locked, and our limbs entwined. I feel so close to her that I think I might burst with passion, and I want this to last but I know I won't be able to hold off the orgasm that's threatening to take over.

"Come with me," Kameron says, and I know she's close too by her quick breaths and the way her body tenses. Only seconds later, we both cry out, clinging onto each other as we fall apart. My own climax rushes to my head and makes me tremble all over, but what affects me most is feeling her contractions around my fingers and hearing her muffled moans against my lips. The way she moves and pushes her body into mine, the waves of delight that seem to keep surprising her, and the sense of togetherness, are simply mind-blowing and so raw that nothing is important, apart from right now.

Then, everything goes quiet as we lie still and take each other in. I don't want to pull out and neither does Kameron. Our breaths are in sync, our hearts pounding fast and I can feel its drumming beat against my chest. She nuzzles my neck, and buries her face against my skin, then whispers, "Who are you?"

26

"Can I take you to the airport later?" Kameron hands me a coffee and gets back into bed with me. She scoots close and pulls me in, giving me no chance to actually drink it. "I assume you're going to meet Tessa before you go, but I'd love to drive you there, after." Not that I'm ungrateful but coffee is the last thing on my mind and all I can think of is spending every last second with her in the best of ways.

"Thank you, I'd like that." After last night, her offer fills me with warmth. We made love for hours, and the memory makes me crave her all over again. I know her body now like she knows mine and that's more special to me than she realizes. "Are you not working today?"

"I took the day off so I could say goodbye."

"That's so sweet." I move closer and turn on my side, aligning myself with her body. A sadness settles over me at the thought of leaving her, but I try to hide it with a smile.

"I'll miss you," Kameron's says, and I know she means it. I woke up with her spooning me with her arms around me, and it made me wish I could lie here for a million years.

"I'll miss you too." I hesitate for a moment, then decide now is not a good time to play games. I want to know where I stand, and I want us to be honest with each other if we're going to try and make this work. "So, you're coming to visit me in New York?"

"Of course." Kameron cups my neck and kisses me. She could do that every morning for the rest of my life, and I wouldn't get tired of it. It's like her lips were made for mine, a perfect fit, a perfect spark. "I'll come as soon as I can."

"Good, because I can't wait to show you New York. And my bed," I add with a smirk.

"I'm excited, too. I want to know what your life is like."

"My life is pretty simple, I'm not exactly a party animal. It's fairly quiet, I would say, apart from my family. They can be a little overwhelming, but you won't have to deal with them."

"Well, I just want to hear you sing," Kameron jokes. "I'm a sucker for a good voice and don't shoot me, but I looked you up at work yesterday, so I know you're an amazing singer. We've had your YouTube channel on in the office."

"You didn't." I give her a playful slap and wiggle myself out of her grip to go to the bathroom.

Kameron laughs and I love the full sound that makes me laugh too. "I'm not joking; we were all singing along."

I shake my head amused at her compliment and the doorbell rings just as I'm putting on her robe. "I'll get it," I say, tying it closed. "Unless you want to get dressed?" I don't wait for an answer and head for the door.

"No, wait, Ivy..." There's a serious hint of panic in Kameron's voice but her protest only vaguely registers. This seems like a very safe neighborhood and if someone had bad intentions, it's unlikely they would come in the daytime. "Ivy, wait!"

Her last plea is much louder—in fact, she's yelling at me, but I'm already opening the door to meet the beaming smile of a delivery man. There's a noise coming from the bedroom and I want to tell her that it's okay, that it's just a delivery, but simultaneously, I'm wondering why she's so worried. I can hear the bathroom door slamming as the friendly looking bearded man holds up a box.

"Package for Countess C. Montgomery?" He says in a thick, southern accent, then frowns and reads out the title again. "Hmm... Countess, that's mighty impressive. We don't get many of those around here. Is that you?"

"Countess Montgomery?" I'm staring at him, open-mouthed.

He's looking me over, trying to decide if I'm worthy of a title.

"That's all right; I'll take it." Kameron has come up behind me, wrapped in a towel. She quickly steps in between us and signs for it, then gives him a polite smile. "Thank you." She looks thrown when she walks into the kitchen and drops it onto the kitchen counter. "Fuck. That wasn't supposed to arrive until tomorrow."

"Sure. And I wasn't supposed to see it, am I right?" My voice is cold and I'm so angry that I can't even begin to express how I'm feeling right now. History just keeps repeating itself; clearly, I'm a fool.

"Ivy, I can explain. I was going to tell you..."

"But you didn't?" I turn away from her and go into the bedroom, then frantically search for anything that belongs to me and stuff it haphazardly into my bag. I feel betrayed, lied to, mislead, and the sudden tightness in my stomach makes me feel sick. I can't think and put my dress on back to front. Desperate to get out of here, I don't bother looking for my underwear as I throw my phone into my purse.

"Please don't go. At least let me explain, everything is different now."

"There's nothing to explain. You lied to me. Twice in a week," I add, and walk right past her, ignoring her pleading stare.

"It's just a title." Kameron attempts to grab my arm, but I move away from her. "It means nothing to me."

"Nothing, huh? Then what's the big deal?" I shoot her a sharp look. "This isn't about who you are. I gave you my body, my mind... my trust." I'm wobbly on my feet as I put on my heels and grab my trench coat from the hanger in the hallway. "I let you in! Do you have any idea how hard that is for me?" The suffocating pressure on my chest is growing and I need to get out of here. "I bet you regret throwing away your phone now, huh?" I yell as I slam the door behind me. I know it's petty, but I can't resist another dig.

"Ivy, please!" Kameron's moved to the balcony now and she's yelling so loudly that I'm pretty sure the whole neighborhood can hear her. "Come back and let me explain. I was going to tell you, I promise!"

I ignore her and walk down the road to the spot where I saw cabs waiting last night. Not wanting her to see me cry, I keep my eyes fixed ahead of me and get into the first one I see.

27

"Ivy, what are you doing here so early?" Tessa ushers me in, then winces as she notices my distress. "Hey, have you been crying? What's wrong?"

Wiping at my eyes, I go into her living room, silently cursing when I see Stephanie putting on a T-shirt. From Tessa's messy hair and the robe that she's still tying closed, it's obvious what they were up to before I showed up. "Sorry, am I interrupting?"

"Never." Without asking, Tessa fetches glasses and pours me a glass of wine, then holds up the bottle to Stephanie. It's not even midday, but she shrugs.

"Sure." Stephanie studies me and shuffles on the spot. "Or do you want me to leave? I totally understand if you prefer that I'm not here." She hesitates. "Is it Kameron?"

"Yeah." I fall back on the couch and take a long drink of the wine. I suspect it will only make me feel worse; alcohol has never been my friend in miserable situations, but I need something, anything to distract me from the hurt that makes me want to curl up in a corner. "And it's fine. Please stay." Whatever I have to say I'm happy for Stephanie to pass on because I have no intention of talking to Kameron ever again and I want her to feel bad about what she's done. "She lied to me," I say, and swallow hard.

"About what?" Tessa asks, sitting down beside me.

"About who she is." I arch a brow and raise my gaze to meet Stephanie's. "And you know very well who she is." Stephanie is silent as she sits down on a chair, her eyes skittishly darting from me to Tessa and back. "A package arrived today. I guess I wasn't supposed to find out."

"What's going on?" Tessa glances from me to Stephanie and back.

"Kameron is Countess Montgomery," I say, before Stephanie has the chance to stop me.

"What?" Tessa looks heavily confused now. "Are you serious? How?"

I don't answer because I have no idea about the details and again, the room falls silent, until Stephanie finally speaks.

"Ivy, she's still the same person. Just because she chooses not to share who she is doesn't mean she's posing as someone else. She's still Kameron. And she's totally into you. I swear, I've never seen her like this with anyone."

"It doesn't matter. I gave her my body and my mind. I trusted her and she shouldn't have lied about something so big. Not after everything we've done together."

"I understand." Stephanie pauses. "Will it make a difference if I tell you that I'm the only person in her life who knows about this? And you and Tessa now," she adds. "Kameron's not in contact with old high school friends anymore. I guess you could say that she started over after her parents died. Her title just makes people want to ask questions about her past and her family and that's painful to her."

I listen but I'm unwilling to accept excuses. Of course Stephanie is going to defend Kameron; she's her best friend. "You might think I'm overreacting because Kameron and I have only just met, but it doesn't feel that way. I'm hurt... It was intense, you know? And it didn't feel that casual anymore." I sigh. "Not after last night, anyway."

"I don't think it was casual to Kameron either." Stephanie takes a sip of her wine. "Maybe you should talk to her, let her explain."

"No. I don't want to see her anymore. I put all my trust in her and I feel... I don't know. Betrayed I guess."

Stephanie nods. "Just think about it, okay? I understand, believe me, I do. But Kameron's a good person. She generally doesn't get close to people but when you have her, you have her for life. She's loyal like that."

Tessa, who has been listening to us, tops up my wine-glass that is still half full. I know she's just trying to help, but as expected, the wine is only making me feel worse, so I ignore it.

"Does that mean you work for Kameron?" she asks Stephanie.

"Yes, I do." Stephanie sits back and props her feet underneath her. "I handle the bookings for the mansion and some other properties she owns and rents out, I organize parties and I manage the charities her family is linked to. She wants to keep them going in memory of her parents, but she's distanced herself from everything, so she doesn't have to parade around, playing the role of an heiress. It was hard for her; she'd only just turned eighteen when it happened and she joined the army as a form of escape, I suppose." She pauses and lets out a deep sigh, seemingly deciding she might as well explain the whole thing as the secret is already out. "When we threw the first women-only party, it was my idea to use her full title for the invitations, but neither of us had expected it to become such a big deal and..."

"And now she's even more protective about her identity because it got out of hand," I say. I purse my lips and give Stephanie a small smile. "I get that. And she's lucky to have you as a friend. Maybe I should have listened to her before I stormed out, but I can't change how I feel right now. I'm just angry and feel like she's deceived me." Deep down, I understand where Stephanie is coming from. Kameron is entitled to her privacy. But because of our conversation last night, and because of the closeness I felt when we were lying in each other's arms this morning, I still think she should have told me who she really was. She had every chance to do so and if we were going to be dating, I think I deserved to know the truth.

"Do you want me to drive you to the airport?" Stephanie asks. "My car is here."

"No, thank you. It's very kind of you, but I'll call a cab." I get up and start gathering the rest of my things, not caring if I miss anything. The gloom is real; I recognize it all too well and I know it's not going to pass anytime soon. I swore I would never be fooled again, but Kameron did just that, and although we weren't that serious, I'd rather cut her off now, than suffer through worse later.

At least I caught the lie this time, and that makes me feel a little better as I zip up my suitcase and stare at my broken expression in Tessa's hallway mirror.

Man up, Ivy. You don't need her.

28

It's been a long week, and singing has not given me the energy it usually does. I'm okay pretending on stage though, and as I've been singing blues, it doesn't matter if my sadness rings through in my voice; it only adds to the drama.

I thought it would be easy—that my anger would help me forget about her—but it's not easy. Memories keep coming back to me, no matter how hard I try to block them, and I constantly see her face before me. It's like she's consumed me and I'm unable to function without her. Hoping this sorrow fades is all I can do.

"Ivy?" My mother nudges me. "Ivy, where has your mind been today?" Her heavy Queens accent and nasal voice blast over the noise of the dryer as I look up to meet her eyes in the mirror. I'm in her salon, having a wash and blowout. It's our weekly catch-up, and the only time we see each other one-on-one. Our family lunches every other Sunday are so chaotic and rowdy that we hardly get to speak, and Brooklyn is somehow an alien concept to her; she rarely ventures out of Queens to visit me.

She's giving me way too much volume, which she knows I don't like but I don't have the energy to argue with her today, so I let her.

"Well?" She switches off the blow-dryer and fusses over some products in the trolley next to her.

"It's nothing," I say, flattening my hair with the palm of my hand when she's doing the final touches, using a ton of lacquer, which I hate, too. The smell is making me nauseous and I hold my breath, wondering how long it would take for me to pass out if she doesn't stop spraying soon.

"Stop that. You're ruining it." She slaps my hand away. "Now tell me, what's up? I'm your mother; I deserve to know."

I let out a deep sigh and take a sip of the strong, bitter coffee that makes some people leave the salon looking like they're on acid. The flavor sooths me though; it tastes like home, and I've gotten used to it. "I don't want to talk about it, and I promise you I'll be back to my old self soon." I don't sound too convincing but that's okay; I can distract her with a question, because she loves to gossip. "How's Aunt Lucia?"

"How's Aunt Lucia?" She repeats my words with an accusing glare. "You mean you haven't spoken to her yet?" My mother starts back-combing my hair, taking advantage of my complacent state. I wouldn't be surprised if she's planning on styling it into a beehive, mirroring her own extravagant updo, but if she does, I'll deal with it when I get home.

"No, I've been busy," I lie.

"Well, she's not great, I can tell you. She has to keep one eye shut for a whole week; they've bandaged her up. Do you have any idea what that does to your balance? She keeps tipping over and..."

The ring of my phone interrupts her, and when I see it's an out of state number, I jump out of the chair and head outside, ignoring her protests. With my cape still on, I rush around the corner and lean against the backdoor of the salon. Seeing as I told myself I never wanted to speak to Kameron again, I can hardly believe how eager I am to hear her voice. I've thought about what Stephanie told me and although I feel a little foolish for creating such drama, I still feel hurt. That doesn't take away the fact that I miss her though, and the flutter in my belly doesn't lie either; I want to talk to her more than anything.

I'm not even sure if it's Kameron, but I pick up anyway.

"Ivy?"

"Hey." I close my eyes, luxuriating in the soothing sound of her deep voice.

"Thank you for picking up." Kameron swallows hard and hesitates. "How are you?"

"Kind of sucky,' I say. "I've been better."

"Yeah, me too." She clears her throat and I'm not sure if she's waiting for me to start shouting at her again. I won't; this moment suddenly feels too precious to waste on angry words. "I'm so sorry about what happened. You may not believe me, but I was going to tell you. I was just waiting for the right moment."

I'm not sure why, but something in her voice makes me believe her, and I'd be lying if I said I wasn't secretly hoping she'd call me. "You hurt me."

"I know. And I'm so, so sorry."

"Maybe I should have given you a chance to explain yourself," I hear myself say and roll my eyes at what a sucker I am. Just hearing her voice is enough for me to forgive her, apparently. "I talked to Stephanie. She told me you don't like to be reminded of your past; that you'd rather just live a normal life, under the radar. I understand that."

"Thank you. But I get why you were angry too. What we

had was... special. And I know you don't just let anyone in." She lets out a deep sigh. "I miss you."

"I miss you too."

"Ivy, what are you doing back there?" It's my mother, waving at me from the door with the can of lacquer still in her hand. "You can't stand out there with your cape on, looking like an idiot. At least let me take it inside."

"Mom, wait!" I hold up my hand to stop her and miraculously, she doesn't come closer. "Can I call you back when I get home?" I say quietly.

"Yes, anytime." Kameron sounds happy, and it makes me smile. "Please, anytime you want, day or night, and I'll tell you anything you want to know. Anything."

"Okay." My smile widens and the gloomy feeling and anxiety that has been sitting in the pit of my stomach all week suddenly lifts like it was never there. "I'll call you soon."

29

———

Despite the grumpy faces, the cold weather, the smell of garbage everywhere, the extortionate cost of living and heavy traffic, New York has always been a warm blanket to me. I grew up here, and it's where I feel at ease, where I can disappear into the crowds and be anonymous yet feel welcome at the same time. I live far enough from my family to avoid them when they all become too much, yet I'm close enough to see them whenever I want, and although I miss having Tessa around the corner, I have some good friends here, who I really cherish.

I usually like my commute to work; the subway is not as busy at night and it gives me time to mentally prepare for my gigs, but today I feel a little flat as I walk the short route from the subway station to the club I'll be singing at. It's strange how missing someone can put a dampener on everything, and sometimes it feels like my life has been covered in a layer of mist, drawing the color out of my surroundings.

As soon as I got home from the salon two weeks ago, I

called Kameron back, and we talked for hours until we both fell asleep on the phone. I asked her a million questions and she told me anything I wanted to know, without hesitation. Since then, we've video called each other every morning. I wake her up and we have our first coffee together, because our schedules are too hectic at night, with me singing and her working. It's cute to see her all sleepy and doing mundane things like making coffee and checking her emails. We talk about anything and everything and that hour is my favorite time of the day. How was your night? Did you dream? Busy day ahead? She tells me about her job and the events, about her colleagues, her friends, and anything that's happened in town. I tell her about my life in return and in the mornings, it's almost like she's there with me.

Never having been a morning person, I'm surprised by how easily I wake up, eager to see her gorgeous smile that kick-starts my day like nothing else. Unlike the evenings, the mornings are real. There's no hiding in the light and I'm totally at ease and myself with her. The only downside of video calls is that it makes me miss her physically. We flirt a lot and sometimes I wear very little, enjoying her burning eyes on me, but it's not a game. We can't get sucked into bed or get caught up in a make-out frenzy and although that's frustrating, it means that we're getting to know each other on a whole new level. I want her to come here but she might think it's too soon since I've only just returned to New York myself.

This morning, she didn't answer, and it clouded my mood. Apparently, her phone was on silent and she didn't hear my call. It's like I need my daily fix of her now, and without it, everything is just flat. She messaged me around midday, apologizing for oversleeping but by now, I'm physically longing to hear her voice.

I feel my phone vibrate and smile when I see I have a message from her. *'Sorry about this morning. I miss you,'* it says, followed by a flame and a heart emoji. Already, I feel a little better, and I message her back while I walk to the staff entrance of the private members' club in Manhattan, where I sing every last Friday of the month.

The jazz club on a quiet corner in the Theatre District is quite an establishment in New York. It's been here since the sixties and the clientele consists of an eclectic mix of old school music lovers, celebrities, bohemian youngsters, artists and other creatives. There's never a dull night here, and it's my favorite place to perform. The stage is fairly small but big bands tend to gather around it or simply blend in with the audience.

Tonight, it's just me and a pianist, which I like. It's intimate and pretty special when the room falls completely quiet and I get to see the faces of the patrons as they look up at me enraptured—completely spellbound by my voice—gathered around rows of small tables that form a half circle around the stage. The lights are dimmed and Roddy, my pianist is already here, warming up his fingers and running a sound check.

"Ivy, good to have you back," he says, and gets up to give me a hug. "How was New Orleans? I bet you saw some amazing bands out there."

"I did," I lie, because I can't exactly tell him that I spent most of my time in bed with another woman. "It was great, can't wait to get back. Are you ready for tonight?"

"Born ready." He points to the microphone. "I sound-checked it for you, but you might want to give it a short run-through to see if you're happy with it."

"I will, Roddy. I'll be ten minutes, just need to get dressed." I cast him a smile over my shoulder and make my way to the dressing room. It's dusty and smells like liquor-soaked carpet but that's nothing new. Most dressing rooms in clubs are low on the renovation lists and are usually neglected by the cleaners too, but the look of faded glory comforts me. Some lamps around the large mirror are broken, the once luxurious wallpaper is peeling off, and the leather of the main dressing room chair is cracked. Sequined dresses, hats and props are hanging from the many hooks on the wall, tagged with the names of the artists they belong to. Anything too big or too fragile to take back and forth on the subway is kept here, adding to the room's ambience—the smell of musky unwashed garments hanging in the air. A red velvet throw covers an old couch and there's a small fridge with beer and water in the corner, buried under a pile of feather boas. I walk over to the hidden liquor stash behind the couch and pour myself two fingers of whiskey, then down it before I put on my black, sequined dress. I have a couple, but this is my favorite. The low back and high side slit are very sexy, and it makes me feel confident on stage.

My hair and makeup are already done. I curled my hair at home, and the dark waves are bouncing over my shoulders when I shake it out in front of the mirror. Just before I go out for the final sound-check, I apply a generous layer of red lipstick and give myself another good glance-over. This theatrical, highly made-up, appearance is not entirely me, but it's what people expect from a jazz singer, and I like giving the audience what they want. Anyway, by now, I've spent so many nights looking like this that the lines have started to blur, and I often find myself putting red lipstick on in the morning, which is something I would have never done ten years ago. I suppose all performers merge with their alter egos at least a little; it's inevitable when you're playing a role for a living.

As I slip into my heels and make my way out onto the stage, my thoughts are with Kameron, and already, I wish I could fast-forward to tomorrow morning, when I'll see her face again.

30

It's our last song of the night. *Black Coffee* is a hard song to sing, but with Roddy's skillful fingers dancing over the piano keys, it always pours out of me easily. We've performed together so many times that it's effortless now, and the six years of bickering behind the scenes have led to a flawless, easy going and intuitive collaboration in which we can try out new things together and improvise without feeling anxious about it. I belt out the last chords, then ease it out and blend in with the soft notes of the piano.

There's always applause at the end but the enthusiasm seems louder tonight. Normally, people are pretty tipsy by midnight and talk through the last songs but tonight there's an appreciation in the audience that surprises me, and I make an extra effort to look at each and every person in front of me, expressing my gratitude with a beaming smile. These are the nights I live for, when everything goes well, and the atmosphere is just perfect.

As my gaze wanders over the second row, my heart jumps at seeing a familiar face. The woman—the only one who has stood up from her chair—is clapping and cheering.

I can barely contain my excitement, and when our eyes meet, she gives me a playful wink and makes her way to the stage.

"Kameron," I stammer, trying to find my voice. I step down and fall into her arms. She hugs me tight but makes no effort to kiss me; I assume she thinks that might be a no-go in here, so I run my hands through her hair and marvel at her handsome face before I lean in to brush my lips against hers. No one is paying attention anymore, and people here simply don't care. She parts her lips and pulls me closer, and it's hard to describe how good it feels to kiss her again. To have her body pressed against mine and to feel the need in her embrace. "How...?"

"You told me you were singing here tonight, so I flew over to watch you." She looks me up and down and licks her lips, and her smile makes me ache. "You look incredible and you were amazing."

"Thank you." I feel myself blush and our electric eye contact sends a rush down my spine. "I can't believe you're here." Leaning in to kiss her again, I take in her scent and the sensation of her hair running through my fingers. I've missed this so much, and the flutter her mouth causes almost makes me forget where I am.

"There was a last-minute cancellation, so I thought I'd surprise you." Kameron tilts her head and looks me up and down when I step back and try to compose myself. My chest is heaving fast and I'm so happy and aroused that I hardly know what to do with myself. "I hope you don't mind. If you have plans, I can keep myself busy."

"I have plans, all right." I pull her along into the dressing room. "But they involve you and me, so I hope you still have some energy left after your long trip."

Kameron laughs. "Hey, in case you've forgotten, I'm a

phantom." She glances at her watch. "I wander at night and I'm looking forward to having my ghostly way with you in a dark room soon."

I smile at her foolishness but indulge her nevertheless. "Good. Because there's a dark room right here." I close the door behind us and lock it. "And you can start by helping me out of this dress."

"I like your plan." Kameron lifts the hem and pulls it up over my head, leaving scratches where the sequins have dragged over my skin.

"That's better." I roll my shoulders that are stiff from the tight dress and let out a sigh of relief as I carefully hang it up and pin my name tag on. I never wear a bra under this dress, and I'm left standing in only my panties.

"You're right. I like the dress, but this is even better." Kameron's hands trace my shoulders and her eyes meet mine while they wander down to my breasts and skim my nipples.

Taking in a quick breath, I inch closer, aware of the desire in my gaze. "Roddy... my pianist... he might come in for a drink. He always knocks first, though."

Kameron grabs hold of my waist and spins me around, so I come face to face with my own reflection in the mirror. "Don't worry; I'll leave if he drops by." Her smile is full of mischief as she stares at me in the mirror and places my hands on the back of the chair in front of me. "I've had this fantasy, you see, and it involves you and me in this dressing room..."

I don't think I've seen myself like this before; so carnal and kind of dirty. My lipstick is smudged from our kiss and my breasts bounce as she slams her hand on my behind. It's unexpected and hard, and I flinch, holding in a cry and a moan at the same time. I doubt anyone can hear us in here, with the music blasting in the bar area, but I don't want to risk it.

Scraping her nails over my back, Kameron pushes me forward. "Fuck, you look so hot like this," she mutters. "Tell me what you want."

"I want you. I want you to take me." Another slap on my ass, and I groan. My pussy is dripping wet now, and I can't wait for her to own me. There's something about seeing us in the mirror that drives me wild. Her bewildered look, filled with dark desire for me, my own raw need, seeping through my gaze.

Kameron's eyes settle on something in our reflection and her lips curl up into a smile. "What's this?" She turns around, takes the riding crop off the wall and studies it.

"That's Mrs. Marvelous' prop," I say through quick breaths. "She doesn't like people touching her stuff." A twitch shoots between my legs at knowing what's about to happen. I'm craving this so much it hurts.

"That's too bad, because I'm going to borrow it anyway."

I brace myself for the crop and when it lands on my behind, a delicious sting spreads out over my skin, making me buck my hips forward.

"Nah-ah. Don't move." Kameron whispers her command in my ear as she pulls my head back by my hair, and I can see her wicked grin in the mirror. The hint of amusement on her face is beyond sexy. She looks devilishly handsome in her sharp, black suit, and the way she controls me without taking it too serious makes me want her even more.

A gasp passes my lips as she wedges her fingers under the edge of my panties and enters me without warning. It's incredibly good to feel her again, to have her fill me up, and when she starts fucking me, I never want her to stop.

"God, you're wet." Her lips part and a frown appears

between her brows, telling me she's been desperate to be inside me. "You feel so good, Ivy."

I moan, then let out a cry as she spanks me again with the crop, twice in quick succession. My skin is burning from the latter that was much harder than the first.

"Black?" she asks with a chuckle when my eyes widen, and I shake my head.

My knuckles turn white from clamping my hands around the back of the chair and I'm fighting to keep my eyes open as her thrusts bring me to the edge of an orgasm. The crop hits me again, and again, while she moves in and out of me, quicker now, pushing her hips into my behind. The sharp stings, the delicious sensation of her skilled fingers and the sight of her aroused expression make me delirious. My moans become louder, and right now, I don't care if anyone can hear me.

"Come for me," she says, and I let go.

"Yes!" My voice is deep and throaty as I push myself back against her while my walls clench around her fingers. She puts an arm around my chest and raises me, so my body is aligned with hers and keeps drawing aftershocks out of me while burying her face in my neck, inhaling deep. I lace my hands through her hair behind me and cherish the closeness as I try to steady my breathing. By the time she pulls out of me, I'm dizzy and feeling a little disoriented. "You're incredible."

"No, you're incredible."

I turn around and kiss her softly, and she takes me in her arms. Nothing has changed apart from one thing: she feels like home.

31

"Nice apartment." Kameron looks around, taking in my spacious loft. The only reason I was able to afford it was because it was falling apart but now it looks just the way I wanted it; clean and cool, mostly white, apart from the original bricks that make up the back wall, and the heavy beams in the exposed ceiling. I love the high, almost cathedral-like ceiling, and the sense of space it gives off. The squatters who were living here before me had made a bedroom in the attic, but I've had everything removed, creating an open and airy apartment.

"My brother Eddie works in construction," I say. "He helped me fix it up."

"That's nice of him. He did a great job."

"Yes, he's awesome. I don't see him enough these days. We used to go out a lot together, but he and his wife had twins last year and moved to the suburbs so nowadays, we only meet during family lunches."

"I didn't know you had nieces." Kameron tilts her head and studies a photo of me cuddling two babies dressed in matching pink dresses. "After all those conversations we had since you left."

"No, I guess I forgot to mention that." I smile. "There's a lot about me you don't know, but now that you're here, you're about to find out." Knowing that Kameron's family died in an accident, I didn't really want to bring up the subject of family, so I've mainly kept my side of our conversations to work and friends.

"I'd like that." Kameron takes off her blazer and hangs it over a kitchen chair, then walks over to the windows that look out over a small park. "Do you come from a big family?"

"Yes. Being third generation Italian, you know..." I shrug. "It's a cliché, but it's true. I have three older brothers and a younger sister. We're all pretty close and we meet up for lunch at my parents' house every other week. My mom's big on Sunday lunch."

"Nice." Kameron twirls a lock of my hair around her finger and I only then realize how much I've missed that simple action. "Are you meeting them tomorrow? Because I don't want to mess up your plans. As I said, I can keep myself busy. I can even get a hotel room if you prefer that; I just wanted to see you."

"There's no way I'm going to let you leave my side." I pull her toward the bed and start unbuttoning her shirt. "I can cancel tomorrow or..." I hesitate, because I know it's a little too soon to introduce her to my family, but I don't want her to think that she's not welcome either. "Or you could come with me? Only if you want to, of course, no pressure," I hastily add, then shake my head. "You know what? I'm sorry, I shouldn't have suggested that, it was silly of me."

Kameron reaches out to stroke my face. "No, it's not silly. I'd be honored. But do your parents even know you're gay?"

"Yeah, they know. And they're cool with it. Or as cool as Italian Catholics can be," I joke. "Seriously, I'd love for you to come with me, but please don't feel pressured. I can cancel, it's not a problem." I don't mention that I've never brought a woman home, or that my parents have never even met one of my girlfriends. Although I haven't thought this through and this is a spur of the moment decision, it feels right, and even if what is happening between us doesn't work out, Kameron is special to me and I'd like my family to meet her.

"Italian Catholics. That sounds pretty daunting for someone like me. I mean, you're so feminine and I'm well..." she laughs. "Let's face it, I'm kind of butch. Do you not think they'll be a little shocked?"

"I think they'll be pleasantly surprised at how wonderful and charming you are" I wink as I slide her shirt off her shoulders. "And one thing's for sure; you'll love my mother's cooking."

"I have no doubt about that." Kameron pulls off my cardigan and my dress and I shriek as she lifts me and carries me to the bed that is standing under a half moon-shaped window at the other end of the loft. "But we'd better not tell your parents what we've been up to."

"What do you mean?" I giggle as she moves back and crosses the room to get her duffel bag. The woman certainly travels light, and I can hardly believe she's managed to stuff everything she needs in there.

"I brought a little something with me," she says, taking the bag to the bathroom.

I lie still and wait in anticipation. My body's been a hot mess ever since she surprised me at the club, and even our dressing room shenanigans haven't stopped the aching need between my legs.

When she appears again, my lips part at the sight of her wearing a strap-on. She's naked and walking toward me with such confidence that I have to squeeze my thighs together to soothe the agonizing pulse that starts there. I'm incredibly aroused and she knows it.

"I couldn't pack much, so I had to choose," she says with a crooked smile. "I want to fuck you, Ivy. Is that okay?"

"Yes," I say in a breathless whisper. "I..." I'm silenced by her mouth on mine and when she lowers herself on top of me, I groan in delight, elated to feel the sensation of her weight on me again.

"I almost forgot how good this felt," she says, mirroring my thoughts. "How good *you* feel." Her delicious lips move to my neck, burning into my skin and I instinctively spread my legs and move my head to the side to welcome her mouth. She sucks at my neck until I'm squirming, my body begging for more.

"Lie down on your back," I say when I turn my head back to meet her eyes. I see them darken as immense arousal flashes through them. I know that look; she wants this more than I do, if that's possible.

Kameron rolls off me and I raise myself over her on my knees that feel weak like jelly. She takes my hips and positions me above the dildo, her chest heaving fast as I slowly lower myself onto it.

I flinch as it glides inside me, its girth stretching me open, but it also feels incredible and I continue until I'm entirely filled up and straddling her. Letting out a long breath, I start rotating my hips, getting used to it as I watch her pant and moan, stimulated by the friction it causes. I know the sight of me on top of her drives her wild, and I've been fantasizing about this myself. Changing my movements, I shift back and forth, arching my back each time I thrust into her, and it hits in the spot where I need it most.

Kameron raises her hips to meet my thrusts, and our eyes lock as I ride her faster, chasing release for both of us. The animal in me is controlling my actions, the side of me that only Kameron can entice to come out and play. This carnal creature isn't me, yet it is.

"Jesus, Ivy..." Her eyelashes flutter and her nails are digging into my thighs as she groans loudly. "Don't stop." She moves a hand to my pussy and rubs her thumb over my clit until I'm shaking heavily, bursting into an orgasm, cursing as I drag her with me.

When I'm finally able to think and breathe again, I fall over her and bask in the delightful closeness of her skin. She takes a tight hold of me and I smile as I bury my face in her neck. I can feel her pulse there, beating hard and fast and the steady thump sooths me like a warm bath.

Looking up, I reach out to touch her face. Even in the dark, she looks like sunshine.

32

"There seems to be a pattern here, us seeing the sun rise together," Kameron murmurs as we're sitting on the top steps of the fire escape, both with a cup of chamomile tea in our hands.

She's wrapped herself in my fluffy white robe and I'm wearing my old college hoodie that I tend to live in when I'm at home.

I've covered the base of the fire escape outside my apartment with Astroturf as I like to sit here in the mornings and watch the neighborhood wake up. We're not really supposed to, but my neighbors below have done the same and even added some plants to the mix. "Are you cold?"

Kameron shakes her head and smiles. "No, this is amazing. And I feel like I have a better idea of you now."

I lean into her and take a sip of my tea. We haven't slept yet, too busy making up for lost time, losing ourselves in each other. The first slithers of light cast an orange glow over the walls of the adjacent brownstones overlooking the small park, where birds are announcing the start of a new day.

I love the mornings here; they're so peaceful. Some of the early dogwalkers are already out, and a couple of night owls are returning home from a party, I'm guessing from their tipsy state and the way they're dressed.

A pigeon lands on the railing and Kameron throws a couple of crumbs from the plate of cookies sitting between us.

"That's Barry. He's tame; he'll eat from your hand." I break a piece off the last cookie and hold my hand out as Barry lands by my feet and lets me stroke him before he scoffs it up.

Kameron laughs. "You're so cute. I thought you said you didn't have pets."

"Just Barry. He's extremely low maintenance and I share the responsibility with the neighbors," I joke. "His girlfriend comes over too, sometimes, but she doesn't like me very much. I think she might be jealous."

"Of course she's jealous." Kameron nudges me. "A gorgeous singer with access to chocolate-chip cookies... Who could resist that?" She turns to me, inhales against my hairline and places a soft kiss on my temple. "In all seriousness though, you seem to have a good thing going on here. Ever thought of moving away?"

"Sure, I've thought about it. Being a singer, I could work almost anywhere in the world, providing I had a buffer that enabled me to build up a network for the first two months or so, but I've never seriously considered taking the big step because in the end, I love New York and my family is here," I say. "On the other hand, New York is very hectic. I mean, it might be peaceful sitting here and watching the neighborhood wake up, but the reality is that you have to face traffic and the subway and the crowds during rush hour. And then there are the hordes of tourists in summer and over the holidays, the high crime rates, and it's expensive. I liked New Orleans and how easy going and happy it was. Southerners seem to enjoy life more, and Tessa loves it there."

"Do you speak to her a lot?" Kameron asks.

"Almost every day. She's smitten with Stephanie; I don't think she's ever been so happy."

"Steph is pretty happy too. I think those two have met their match." Kameron's gaze dips to my lips, and I'm unable to resist stealing a kiss. "She told me I was foolish to come here without giving you notice. Said it might freak you out."

"Not at all. It was the best surprise." I smile. "I like surprises."

"I'll keep that in mind."

I take Kameron's hand and squeeze it. "What about you and that huge mansion of yours? You told me it belonged to your grandfather. Would you ever consider moving in there?"

Kameron nods. "I thought about fixing it up and moving in there when I inherited it, but the idea of living in that big house by myself creeped me out, so after much deliberation, I decided to sell it. Steph convinced me it would be a great place to throw a women-only party before I put it up for sale and I liked the idea. It turned out to be a huge success—you know the story by now—and that got me thinking it could be a commercial goldmine. So, now I'm renting it out for corporate events and four times a year, I throw a party there myself. I never meant for my name to become so legendary in the city. I just wanted to stay anonymous, initially, you know, because of the nature of the parties. But then people started talking and before I knew it, Countess Montgomery was this mysterious figure.

"What about your team? They know your surname, right? Has no one ever figured it out?"

"No, they haven't. But Montgomery is not an unusual surname and rumor has it that the Countess is this extravagant lady who's into witchcraft and voodoo—God knows how that manifested, but you know how it goes when people start to gossip. Also, there is the assumption that the Countess is straight, as that title can generally only be acquired through marriage in the US, so that makes it even more unlikely that they'd link me to her."

"I was wondering about that. How did it work with you?"

"As you know, my family is from Scottish descent," Kameron says. "And in Scotland, a title can be passed on to the eldest son, and in the absence of a son, to a daughter. My brother was supposed to be the next Earl, but since he died in the accident, the title went to me." There's a hint of sadness in her voice as she mentions her family, but she composes herself and shoots me a grin. "Frankly, I think people might be terribly disappointed if they found out it was me."

"I doubt they would." I kiss her and when I close my eyes, I suddenly feel how tired I am. We haven't slept yet and I suspect Kameron is exhausted too, as she pulls back and yawns.

"We should probably get some sleep if we're seeing your parents later today," she says as she gets up and holds out a hand to help me up too.

"Yeah." I leave the last crumbs of the cookies outside for Barry and sigh in delight as we crawl under the covers together, snuggling up close. My bed has never felt so good as now, with her in it.

33

_____

"Are you still up for this?" I ask as we stand in front of my parents' house. They still live in the same small two-story house that I grew up in. It's got a funny wooden yellow outbuilding at the front, and I don't get why they keep painting it that color, drawing attention to the bad architecture.

"I think so." Kameron laughs as she pulls me closer to put me at ease. "I can't say I've ever met anyone's parents before, but there has to be a first time for everything, right?" She winks. "Seriously though, I'm fine. I just hope they don't..."

"Ivy!" my mother interrupts us as she opens the door. I've called ahead to let her know I was bringing a date. She sounded surprised and a little thrown at first, and I was worried she might not want to face the reality of my sexuality after all. Saying you're okay with it is one thing, but being confronted with it is another, so I was actually relieved when she scolded me for not letting her know sooner, so she could prepare something special for the occasion. Then she fired off a million questions that I was unable to answer because I'm not sure how much Kameron wants strangers to know about her, since she's so private. I should have warned her about how nosey my mother is, but it's too late now, and I'll just have to hope for the best.

"Hi, Mom, it's good to see you." I give her a hug and two kisses. "This is Kameron."

My mother shamelessly looks Kameron up and down, and I can tell Kameron is getting a little uncomfortable. Finally, she gives her a beaming smile and pulls her into a tight hug too. "Welcome, honey. It's so good to finally meet one of Ivy's romantic friends."

I chuckle at her choice of words but don't comment. If that's what she wants to call it, that's fine with me and so far, it's not so bad for a first meeting. Frankly, I'm so nervous I can barely hold myself up, but Kameron doesn't need to know that.

"It's lovely to meet you too, Mrs. Giacometti." Kameron hands her a bottle of wine and is ushered in.

I'm so used to coming home that I'd forgotten how daunting it must be to walk into my parents' small and extremely noisy dining room, where thirteen people are cramped around the long dining table, talking, laughing and arguing. My parents, my grandmother, my three brothers and their wives, the twins, who are usually screaming all through dinner, my sister and her boyfriend, and their two dogs who constantly try to steal food from the table. The eighties decor is dated and totally uncoordinated, but I love this room. It's where I've had the best times of my life, enjoying my mother's food with my chaotic family.

Everyone falls silent as we walk in, and the noise of the TV in the adjacent living room is the only sound left as everyone holds their breath, staring at us. I decided to arrive late on purpose, to give my mother time to tell them that I was bringing someone with me. Since they were going to gossip anyway, I'd rather have them do it before we arrived.

"Come on guys, this is weird," I say, rolling my eyes at them before I greet everyone and introduce Kameron. "Please continue whatever you were talking about."

"We can't. We were talking about you," my sister Erin says, and the laughter that follows takes away some of the awkwardness in the room. "So, you finally brought a girl-friend home." She gets up to pull Kameron into a hug. "I thought Ivy was just gay for attention but here you are. How come you never told me about her, sis?"

"We only met last month," I say, then shoot my sister a warning look, letting her know to hold off on the gay jibes. She's the worst and although I know she's only joking, I've been called just about every rainbow insult under the sun since I came out at seventeen.

If Kameron is fazed by the crowd, she doesn't let it show and she's as charming as always, making small talk with Eddie and complementing him on his work on my apart-ment. She's good with children too, I notice, as she's making the twins—who are usually unbearable at the table—giggle and shriek when she kneels down to tickle them.

Noting my mother is beaming, I feel like I can breathe again. My father is a little standoffish, but that's nothing new so I don't take it personally, and my grandmother, who has never accepted that I'm gay, has probably convinced herself it's just a phase or that Kameron is just a friend. It's all good and I pat the chair next to me as I sit down.

I pour red wine for us while my mother dishes out antipasti and just like that, things are almost back to normal. I say almost, because my mother won't stop staring at us—this curious frozen grin on her face—and it's highly awkward.

Kameron takes a bite of the arancini and moans. "This is really, really good, Mrs. Giacometti."

"Thank you. It's my specialty." My mother claps her hands together. "And please call me Bea."

"Mom claims everything is her specialty," I joke and help myself to some pickled peppers.

"Yes, everything on the planet," Eddie chips in. "She knows how to make the best food, where to find the cheapest fabrics, the best beauticians, the most accomplished lawyers—God only knows what she needs them for —and she also claims to be the best matchmaker in history, although none of us have ever successfully been matched up by her, or anyone I know for that matter."

"Hey, what can I say? I do what I'm good at," my mother says in all seriousness, ignoring his dig. "I love feeding and connecting people. I'm a people person and I happen to know about a lot of stuff. They call me the connector around here, you know. The neighbors come to me for advice all the time, no kidding."

I've always thought my mother should have her own reality show. The way she looks—totally over the top with her beehive and rhinestone studded glasses, her fake Versace blouse and the way she speaks with her heavy Queens accent—surely must be amusing to people who aren't familiar with the New York Italian subculture.

"So, tell me about your family, Kameron," she continues while constantly fussing over the food, making sure everyone's plate is filled at all times. "Is it as rowdy as this one? Ivy told me you're from New Orleans. I've never been there but I hear it's a great city. Do they really eat alligator there? Is your ma a good cook?"

As expected, she's started firing off an arsenal of questions and random remarks, and I feel for Kameron. Maybe this was a bad idea. I shouldn't have brought her here because it's sure to bring up memories she'd rather not revisit while meeting her girlfriend's family. My mother lives by the motto that everything should be discussed, no matter how private or painful and that usually leads to awkward situations, emotional outbursts or even fights, at times.

"Not quite. To be honest, I don't think I've ever dined with a big family before. It must be nice to have all your kids close by." Kameron is skillfully surfing around the topic but she's not going to escape the questioning my mother has undoubtedly prepared over the little time she had.

"Yes, it's a blessing to have them all here together regularly but I do want more grandchildren. One of my sisters, Sonya, has five but I've only got two so far." My mother shoots us all a pressing look. "But anyway, your parents..."

I knew she wouldn't give up. "Mom, please stop with the interrogation," I beg her, but she ignores me.

"Tell me, I want to know who my daughter is dating."

Kameron nods, resigned to her fate, and I feel awful because I should have prepared her for this. "My family is not around anymore, actually. My grandparents have passed away and my parents and brother died in an accident twenty-nine years ago, so it's just me and a couple of cousins left, and I'm not really in contact with them."

"Oh, honey, I'm so sorry." My mother's face says more than words ever could. The emotion is real, and for a moment, I'm worried she might start crying and make matters worse. The sudden silence at the table is unbearable and my mind is working overtime, trying to come up with something to say.

"It's okay. I mean, it's not okay, but I'm fine. You don't need to feel sorry for me." Kameron smiles and continues, clearly feeling the need to fill up the silence. "I'm happy with where I am in life."

"Honey, I still feel for you and I want you to know that you'll always be welcome here. Always." My mother places her hands on her heart and it might seem dramatic, but I know she means it. When her neighbor from three doors down died last year, she cried for three weeks, even though she didn't even know him that well.

"Thank you." Kameron takes my mother's hand and squeezes it and that simple gesture brings a lump to my throat. "And to answer your question, no, my mother was not a good cook. In fact, I don't think she ever cooked a day in her life. My brother and I were mostly raised by a nanny, and I've never really lived a typical domestic life, so I'm not the best in the kitchen either, I'm afraid."

"A nanny?"

"Mom thinks nannies are the devil,' my sister jokes in an attempt to ease the mood.

Kameron laughs and shakes her head. "Well, mine was really nice. I'm still in contact with her. She's in a home outside New Orleans now and I still visit her once a month."

This is something I didn't know, and I'm surprised how easily she's opening up to my mother. Perhaps she meant it when she said she didn't want any more secrets between us, and she seems okay talking about herself.

"Why did the nanny raise you?" My mother asks. "Was your mother not home?"

"No, my mother and father ran businesses together and travelled a lot." Kameron hesitates, then says, "I guess you could say they were socialites. They had a lot of commitments because of the charities and companies our family ran."

I see my sister spiking to attention at the word. She's

obsessed with anything glamorous and pursued a career in both modelling and acting before she settled for being a hairdresser, like my mom.

"Were they famous?" she asks.

"Not really, just well-known in certain circles." Erin's eyes shift from my mother to me and back and I jump in.

"You don't have to talk about them if you don't want to," I say, offering help, but my sister raises her voice, drowning out mine.

"What do you mean by that?"

"Seriously, guys! Enough with the questions." I glare at my sister and mother, and they both hold up their hands in apology. My sister's mannerisms have become identical to my mom's over the years, and if this wasn't such a tense subject matter, I would find it funny.

"It's okay." Kameron clears her throat. "They were the Count and Countess of Montgomery," she says. "My family were from Scottish descent. But I generally don't talk about it as I don't lead that life. I prefer to live under the radar, so part of my company now runs the charities and two of my cousins run the businesses that are still under our control."

Again, there's a silence. I imagine this is hard to grasp for my lovely but seriously working-class family. Most of them have never studied, or left the country, let alone met members of the aristocracy. Their all-time idol is our cousin Linda, who was once a contestant on a TV quiz in the nineties. She didn't even win, and she's still considered a celebrity in the family.

"So are you a Countess, too?" my sister asks, now being just as annoying as my mother.

"Technically, yes, but as I said, I don't call myself that. I'm just Kameron. I run a security company, I live in a modest apartment and I love music. Speaking of which...", she continues, turning to me, "I had the privilege of hearing Ivy sing last night and she blew me away. Your daughter is incredibly talented."

"She is." My mother gives me a proud smile and the rest of my family mumbles their agreement. "So..." She waves a finger between me and Kameron. "If you two have kids, will they have a title too?"

Both Kameron and me roar with laughter and shake our heads. I'm grateful for my brothers, who laugh along and finally tell my mother to stop her questioning.

I'm surprised when my father—a man of few words—decides to say something. "Will you leave her alone now, Bea. Why don't you talk about the twins or yourself, or tell her about cousin Linda for all I care? Just give her a break. This is supposed to be a welcoming family dinner, not an interview." He shakes his head incredulously, then focuses on his food again.

We all hold our breath, waiting for my mother to start shouting at him, but instead, she adds something to her plate and gives Kameron a warm smile. "Very well, let me tell you something I think will impress you. Have you ever heard of the TV program *Hundred-Dollar Question*?"

34

"I think that went well," Kameron says as we're waving goodbye to my brother, who has dropped us off at my apartment after the long lunch.

"Really? I assumed it was a nightmare for you." I grimace. "I'm so sorry about my mom and my sister, I should have warned you about them."

"No, it's fine. I like them. They're all super nice and even your grandma who was shooting me funny looks when I arrived, was thawing toward the end." Kameron follows me inside and helps herself to a bottle of water from my fridge. We've had a lot of wine, which isn't unusual for a family lunch, but I suppose the nerves made us both drink a little bit more than we normally would.

"I'm glad you're not traumatized."

"Not in the slightest. It's been really fun and interesting." Kameron smiles at me and hands me the water after taking a sip herself. "It was a first for me; meeting someone's family, but I didn't realize it was a first for you too."

I feel myself blush and look down at my feet. "Yes, it was

a pretty big thing for me, but I didn't want to freak you out by telling you that."

"That's probably a good thing, because you might have freaked me out," she says with a smile. "Not that that would have stopped me from going; I was so curious as to who had raised this wonderful and beautiful creature that I would have followed you anyway."

This makes me blush even harder, and I shuffle on the spot. There's so much I want to say to her but it's harder face to face than over the phone. Having her here has made me realize how compatible we are, how happy she makes me, and how well she slots into my life. She's sweet, funny, generous, respectful, sexy and she gets along with my family. Most of all though, I'm so in love with her that I don't even know how to express it, and I need a moment to find words, any words to try and tell her how I feel.

"Are you okay?" she asks, sensing my hesitation.

"I'm okay." I raise my gaze to meet her eyes. "Listen, I know we haven't known each other for that long, but there's something about you..." I stop myself then. "No, wait, there's a lot about you, about us together, that makes me think this could be something real, and I'm just going to say it. I've thought about nothing else but you since I left New Orleans. Every time you call, it's like my whole world lights up and every second I spend with you is so special and precious that I never want it to end. You have no idea how crazy I am about you."

Kameron stares at me for what seems like an eternity, then closes the distance between us and takes me into her arms. "I'm glad you said that because I never want this to end. I'm so, so head over heels for you too, and honestly, I didn't know this existed. I put the instant chemistry down to physical attraction at first, which it partly was, of course, but

I feel this deep connection with you, something that goes above and beyond the physical and I miss you every second that you're not with me. I don't want to go back tomorrow but unfortunately, work calls." She tightens her grip and squeezes me so hard that I can barely breathe.

"I know." I'm okay with saying goodbye this time, because I'm positive that everything will be fine. This won't fade, and knowing we'll speak to each other every day makes it easier to let her go.

"When can I see you again?" Kameron gives me a smile that carries a hint of humor. "I mean, your mother made me promise to visit more often and how can I say no to that?"

"My mother..." I laugh and shake my head. "And to answer your question, you'll see me whenever you want to see me."

Kameron pauses and for the first time, she comes across as a little shy. "Always, is the answer to that."

"Well then, how about I come over to New Orleans soon?" I look over at the calendar on my fridge, where the dates circled in red indicate my bookings. "In two weeks? Then you can indulge my mother with your presence next time you come here."

"Perfect." Kameron kisses me tenderly, almost lovingly and the swarm of butterflies it sends to my core makes me feel light-headed and intoxicated with longing. Her mask has finally dropped, and there's no front, no disguise. This is real.

EPILOGUE

I t's good to be back in New Orleans and it's hard to believe it was only a year ago that I came here for the first time. I've visited Kameron many times over the past year and she's visited me in New York every month, but this reunion is special.

A lovely couple—my new tenants—moved into my loft last week, and I've shipped all my things over to Kameron's apartment. Yesterday I arrived to find my clothes in the closets, my books on the shelves and my other personal possessions in boxes for me to store away myself. One of Kameron's employees, who sometimes acts as an assistant, has been super helpful and made it so easy that moving didn't feel like a big step at all.

With the vibrant music scene here, I doubt it will be hard for me to find gigs, and I'm excited to explore some new venues. Kameron's contacts will be very useful too, as she knows most of the club owners and people in the industry.

I inhale deeply and take in the scent of my new hometown. It doesn't smell of garbage, but instead, the air is earthy and infused with spices used in the restaurants we're passing.

"Kameron, Stephanie, myself and Tessa are walking to 'Countess Montgomery's' house for one of her masked women-only parties after getting dressed up at Kameron's place, or perhaps I should say, our place, now.

Tessa has been bouncing off the walls since my arrival, planning all the things we're going to do together now that I'm living here, and she hasn't stopped talking since we met tonight.

Kameron is wearing a black suit and the same white phantom mask as last year, and it feels strange yet immensely arousing to see her like this. Stephanie has opted for black again but is now wearing an identical dress to Tessa's. It's long with a high side slit, their hold-ups and garters visible underneath. Seeing Tessa so happy makes my heart melt, and I can hardly believe it's already been a year since we were last here.

My sexy Catwoman-inspired outfit, consisting of shiny black leggings, thigh-high boots and a revealing black top, topped off with a whiskered cat-mask and tail, is without a doubt the most daring thing I've ever worn in public, but it makes me feel good and I love the way Kameron is looking at me.

"Isn't this amazing?" Tessa pulls at my tail, then hooks her arm through mine. "And this time, we won't even have to worry about the password," she adds, then furrows her brow. "What is the password, anyway?"

We've arrived in front of the security gates, and Daisy, the security guard who busted us last year, grins as she over-hears Tessa's question. "Well?" she asks, looking down at Tessa, who only reaches up to her chest. "Don't tell me you're crashing again," she jokes.

"Well?" Tessa laughs and passes the question over to Kameron.

"Ivy," she says, and Daisy gestures for us to walk through.

"Seriously?" Tessa rolls her eyes skyward. "You moved here yesterday and already your name is the password for one of the most anticipated parties of the year. How is that fair?"

I chuckle and hear Kameron whisper something to Daisy before she joins us, but she simply smiles when I shoot her a questioning look.

"It's nothing, don't worry about it, babe."

I don't, because I trust her with my life.

The party is already in full swing when we walk through the doors. The cocktail bar is set up in the same place as last year, with green drinks, this time, and women are dressed to impress and filling the room with sexual tension.

"Do I want to know what's in here?" I joke, as I order a cocktail and clink my glass with Kameron's.

"I can tell you exactly what's in it, but I doubt you'll need it." Kameron pulls me in and gives me a heated kiss that sets me on fire and sends a tingle through my whole body. "You've proven to be more insatiable than me when it comes to the bedroom. I've had a hard time keeping up with you lately."

She's right; since meeting her, my sexual appetite has skyrocketed, and whenever we're together, I seem to be unable to think of little else. I can only hope I won't exhaust her, now that we'll be living together.

Tessa and Stephanie are talking to two other ladies, but I'm not interested in mingling as I suspect it will lead to propositions. This is not for me after all, and I like that

Kameron only has eyes for me. A shiver runs through me when she leans in and brings her mouth close to my ear.

"Will you join me upstairs and let me fuck you senseless?"

Unlike last year, I don't shy away from the question, and I give her a flirtatious smile. "Absolutely." Taking her hand, I let her guide me up the stairs.

We're passing women who are making out, sitting on the steps or leaning against the balustrade, and already, there's an air of sexual tension in the house. I like Kameron in her costume; it turns me on and reminds me of the most memorable night of my life, and I can tell by the hunger in her eyes that she loves my tight outfit too.

When we reach the end of the corridor on the second floor and she unlocks the door, my mouth falls open. I was expecting the same old dusty room as last year, but I hardly recognize it. The walls have been painted a light gray, the bed has been painted white, made up with crisp seersucker bedlinen. There's a new dressing table with a big mirror opposite the bed, and a built-in closet with a floor-to ceiling shoe rack next to it. On the floor are cozy rugs in gray tones, and the chandelier has been cleaned and is now sparkling in the light of the many candles on the windowsills, the dressing table and the nightstands. It's elegant and graceful, but what touches me most are the white rose petals that are scattered over the bed.

"Kameron... This is amazing, when did you do all this?" I turn to her and kiss her.

"Just a little bit here and there, when I had time. Daisy's responsible for the petals and the candles, though. I had a private talk with her yesterday after I decided to trust her with my secret." She looks proud as she continues. "I've been working on it for a couple of months, the bathroom is done, too." She points to the bathroom door and I walk in to find a luxurious white-tiled bathroom with a rain shower and a big, freestanding tub.

"I love it. But why go through all the trouble for only one night? No one ever comes in here, right?"

"True. But I was thinking... what if we fixed up the house? You can help me, and we could make it our own." Kameron grins when my lips pull into a wide smile, because I know where she's going with this now.

"Are you saying what I think you're saying?"

"Yeah, I'd love to live here with you one day, if you want that too. I thought it would be nice to have a bigger place so your family can visit. They must be terribly upset with me for stealing you away from New York."

My eyes well up because that's the sweetest thing she's ever said to me. "That's so thoughtful." I look around the room and can already imagine what the house will look like, restored with modern-day comforts.

"We could even put a pool in the backyard," Kameron adds, as if trying to persuade me. "That would be cool, right?"

There's no need for persuasion. My family aside—whom I'll miss of course, but I hadn't even considered the possibility of them visiting as they rarely venture out of New York—making this our home together is more than I ever could have wished for.

"A pool... " I wrap my arms around her once again and meet her gaze. There's still the lust that always makes me want her, but there's also so much tenderness and love that I have to fight back my tears. I love this woman more than I ever thought I could love someone, and her proposal is so touching that a tear trickles down my cheek. "Although I generally don't care about anything as long as I'm with you,

I love the idea." I hesitate as a thought strikes me. "But wait… people will find out who you are if we move in here."

Kameron shrugs. "They don't have to find out, but if they do, that's a small price to pay." She lifts me up and kisses me hard, and before we know it, we're making out like we haven't seen each other in years. Her hands wander down to my ass and she squeezes my cheeks, making me moan against her mouth while she walks us back toward the bed. "We'd better christen our future bedroom then, Miss Black."

My breath hitches when she backs me up against the bedpost, reminding me of the night we met. She gives me that charismatic smile that usually makes me weak in all limbs, but right now, I tense up instead, anticipation building inside me as she slowly runs a hand up my thigh. "The safe word is 'black'."

AFTERWORD

I hope you've loved reading *Masquerade* as much as I've loved writing it. If you've enjoyed this book, would you consider rating it and reviewing it? Reviews are very important to authors and I'd be really grateful.

ALSO BY MADELEINE TAYLOR

The Good Girl

Online

Santa's Favorite

www.ingramcontent.com/pod-product-compliance
Lightning Source LLC
Chambersburg PA
CBHW050942120626
46552CB00001B/339

*9 7 8 1 8 3 8 1 6 4 3 0 0 *